Bertie's War

Bertie's War

a Novel

Barbara Tifft Blakey

Kregel
Publications

Bertie's War: A Novel

© 2009 by Barbara Tifft Blakey

Published by Kregel Publications, a division of Kregel, Inc., P.O. Box 2607, Grand Rapids, MI 49501.

Published in association with the Books & Such Literary Agency, Janet Kobobel Grant, 52 Mission Circle, Suite 122, PMB 170, Santa Rosa, CA 95409-5370, www.booksandsuch.biz.

Apart from certain historic and public figures and historic facts, the persons and events portrayed in this work are the creations of the author, and any resemblance to persons living or dead is purely coincidental.

Library of Congress Cataloging-in-Publication Data
Blakey, Barbara Tifft.
    Bertie's war : a novel / Barbara Tifft Blakey.
        p. cm.
    I. Title.
PS3602.L3498B47   2009   813'.6—dc22   2008054749

ISBN 978-0-8254-2432-8

Printed in the United States of America
09 10 11 12 13 / 5 4 3 2 1

To Mom, Dad, Debi, and Allan

Chapter 1

𝓕ire!

AAARRRRRRRRR-AAARRRRRRRRRRR!

A fire truck siren jolted me awake from my daydream adventure with Arwen and the other elves in Rivendell. I jumped up from the mossy cushion under the massive dogwood trees and scrambled toward the sound. *Is it coming to our farm or passing by on the highway?*

The screeching grew louder.

A blackberry vine snagged my sweatshirt and a thorn jabbed my bare foot as I picked my way through the thicket, and wiggled under the bottom wire of the electric fence. Near the top of the hill I got the first whiff of smoke. When I rounded the corner of our weatherworn barn, I saw the fire truck. Beyond it, black smoke streamed from the vacant farm workers' housing.

I stumbled against the barn, willing the firemen to kill the fire. "Put it out! Save my house!" I whispered the words over and over as if I were chanting a spell. A splinter from the barn poked through my blue jeans. I inched away from the rough wall, my heart pounding to the rhythm of the words, "Put out the fire! Save my house!"

Long ago during harvest season, migrant workers lived in the long, narrow building that was divided into four homes. For as long as I could remember I had used apartment A as a playhouse. I thought I was the luckiest girl alive. I suspected most twelve-year-old girls didn't still play house—but most twelve-year-old girls didn't have a real house in which to play. And maybe they didn't need one. Maybe they weren't like me.

At a sharp tug on my braids, I whirled around to see my younger brother Aaron with Joel, his friend from across the highway. Joel grinned at me, but Aaron only glanced my way before focusing on the fire. He sniffed and shook his head, muttering, "Boy, am I gonna get it!"

I stared at him. "Did you do that?"

He didn't answer, but gaped at the fire. Joel slipped away.

Hands on hips, facing Aaron squarely, I repeated my question. "Did you start the fire? Why would you do that?"

He still didn't answer, but wiped his nose on the back of his hand, a cigarette clutched between his fingers. *A cigarette?* I looked from his hand to his face. It took only a second for everything to become perfectly clear.

He was gonna get it and get it good.

"Aaron! Roberta!" Mom's frenzied call reached beyond the roaring engine and crackling flames.

"Bertie, get out of the playhouse!" Tami, our older sister, puffed along beside Mom. As a fireman approached them, they pointed toward the burning structure and tried to run past him.

"Mom! Mom, it's all right. We're here!"

Mom and Tami spun toward the sound of my voice. I grabbed Aaron's arm and dragged him with me. As we neared her, Mom smiled, the relief in her eyes a sharp contrast to how I felt. I glanced at the fire. Smoke poured out of doors and windows. Tears streamed as I watched the blaze dance along the roof. *Pleeeease save my house!*

Mom reached out to hug us in one big embrace, but Aaron pulled back, his guilt as plain as a black cow in a green field. His shoulders slumped as he kicked at a dirt clod.

"Look at me, young man."

He kept his head down and his hands behind his back.

Does he still have the cigarette? Why didn't he get rid of it? I knew once caught he wouldn't lie. The last time he had fibbed resulted in a trip to the woodshed, and that took care of that. I'd never heard him lie again.

Mom grabbed his arms, forcing them out from behind his back. He opened one hand, revealing a grimy cigarette.

"Oh, Aaron! What have you done?" Mom's hands dropped to her side. She raised them to cover her face, then planted them on her hips. "I don't know what to do with you! I don't even know what to think! Whatever possessed you to . . . Oh, Aaron, I'm so angry!"

She took the cigarette from his hand, pinching it between her fingers as if it were a nasty bug.

Aaron fumbled in his coat pocket and pulled out a half-empty book of matches. He glanced at Mom's face, but looked down again as she took it from him.

"Come on. Back to the house. Now." Mom spoke in her no-nonsense voice. I sucked on the end of my braid as I watched the flames attack the porch railing. "Mom, can I stay and watch?" I took a deep breath. "It's my playhouse."

"No, I've got bread in the oven and you can't stay alone. I don't want to worry about you getting in the way." She nodded in the direction of the firefighters.

We trudged toward home. I knew she thought the building was an eyesore; I'd heard her and Dad talking about how it wasn't worth even a coat of paint. *Maybe not to them.* I looked back as we neared the porch steps. A cluster of trees hid the fire scene, but smoke rose above them in huge, balloonlike puffs.

Mom placed the cigarette and matches on the table, washed her hands and went to the stove. The smells of beef stew and homemade bread made everything feel normal, as if nothing bad had happened. The feeling lasted only a moment.

I sat at the table by Aaron where I could at least see the fire trucks. A plume of smoke announced to all of Thurston County, Washington, "Fire at the Thorne's!" I could see the headlines in the next *Dale Valley News*: "April 25, 1962, Marks Day Thorne Homestead Burns."

Aaron kicked his feet back and forth hitting the chair leg. Thud. Thud. I waited for Mom to tell him to stop, but she didn't. Thud. Thud. I looked away from the window at my brother. He was small for his age and looked more like Tami than me with his sun-streaked blond hair and spattering of freckles. A deep dimple appeared on his right cheek whenever he smiled, but he wasn't smiling now.

He quit kicking the chair leg and picked up the cigarette. He broke it in half and tiny pieces of brown flakes floated onto the table. *How can you sit there touching that nasty thing after all the damage you've done?* I scooted my chair away from him. This was his fault, and there he sat fiddling with a filthy cigarette.

My playhouse had always been there for me, a refuge for fantasies. Sometimes I was a mom taking care of my babies, sometimes a secret agent on a dangerous mission. In my make-believe worlds I always did and said the right things; there were no Communists or Cubans or threats of nuclear war; my dad never frowned at me; and there was no woodshed, no punishment.

An explosion rattled the windows. *Is that my playhouse?* No one jumped but me, and I should have known better. Nearby Fort Lewis often practiced maneuvers this time of day and their detonations regularly shook the windows, a ready reminder of the probability of war.

"Roberta, get your hair out of your mouth."

As I obeyed, another detonation rattled the windows. A tiny squeal escaped before I covered my mouth with both hands. Tami snickered and Aaron rolled his eyes, but I ignored them.

When Dad's old Studebaker rumbled up the lane, Mom shooed Tami and me from the kitchen. It took awhile for Dad to come into the house; I supposed he had stopped to talk with the firefighters. The screen door banged shut before I heard his footsteps.

Tami and I crouched near the swinging door that separated the kitchen from the dining room. I couldn't make out Dad's words, but his voice was angry.

Tami pushed slightly on the door and we peeked through the crack. Aaron slouched in his chair at the kitchen table, a glass of water in front of him. Dad lit a cigarette and handed it to him. Aaron took it, puffed, coughed.

"I don't want it, Dad."

"Take another drag."

Dad never raised his voice, not at us, not at Mom, not at anyone. It was a terrifying voice nonetheless, deep and gruff and coldly calm. I ached for my little brother as he exhaled a wisp of smoke.

"Take a deeper puff."

Aaron sucked on the cigarette and coughed. Mom handed him the glass of water. When he tried to drink it, he sputtered and gasped.

"Ron, he's only ten. Remember, he's only ten." Mom sat down at the table, her back to us.

Aaron looked up at Dad, his blue eyes wide. "Can we go to the woodshed now, sir?"

Go to the woodshed now? I couldn't believe he said that. I looked at Tami, but she just shrugged. Both Tami and Aaron had been to the woodshed for disobeying or breaking rules. I avoided it by doing everything as right as I could.

Neither my brother or sister talked about what happened to them there, but everyone knows what happens in a woodshed. Once I asked Aaron how much it hurt, but he just shook his head and walked away. I didn't ask him again. As long as I obeyed, as long as I always did the right thing, I'd never have to know.

Chapter 2

Still Standing

THE NEXT MORNING AS I ATE TOAST AND CANNED PEACHES, ALL I could think about was my playhouse. I closed my eyes and willed it to be standing. I pictured it as it had been: sagging porch; weatherworn lap siding; mossy roof; the old, wood cookstove perched in the corner on a scuffed, hardwood floor; yellow, ruffled curtains at the window above the sink; the old, brass bed frame in the bedroom and yellow-flowered wallpaper throughout.

I tried to sneak out before school, but Mom caught me on the porch. "It's raining cats and dogs, Roberta. Stay inside."

After school the rain continued, but when the dinner dishes were done, I ran to the site in the darkening twilight. It was still standing! Apartments C and D were a heap of charred boards, but my playhouse and apartment B had survived. The air smelled of smoke and wet wood, and the blackened porch boards creaked as I stepped on them. I peered through the broken window in the kitchen door. The old stove sat unharmed. The ceiling was sooty, the wallpaper streaked and water-stained, and the floor muddy, but everything else looked fine. As I grasped the doorknob, I heard footsteps grating on gravel. Thinking it was Aaron, I turned, eager to share the good news. Instead of Aaron, I faced Dad's scowl.

"Get off the porch," he ordered. "First breeze to come along and the whole thing will come down. You stay away and I don't mean maybe." Then he grumbled, "They should have let the blasted thing burn."

I turned to go, but stopped. "Dad? Can I get my stuff? It'll only take a minute."

"*May* I, not *can*. And no, you may not. You are never to go in there again. It's ready to collapse."

I shuffled back home. Chilled from the damp, evening air, I plopped on the stool near the trash burner. Mom noticed me sulking in the corner. "Come with me, Roberta."

I followed her outside, past the woodshed to the storeroom. Mom pulled open the heavy door and we went inside. She stood in the middle of the dingy room, her hands on her hips. "Well, what do you think?"

"What do I think about what?"

"It's not a real house, not like your old playhouse, but it has a window, a sink, even electricity."

I looked around. Plywood shelves lined two walls. Canning jars filled with peaches, pears, and green beans stood in perfect formation like rotund soldiers. Canvas tarps covered a large, misshapen heap along the back wall. A light bulb dangled in the middle of the room and a cobwebby window with four cracked panes stood guard over a chipped porcelain sink.

I nodded at Mom. It wasn't much, but it was something. Electricity meant I could use it after dark, something I couldn't do in the old playhouse.

Dad loomed in the doorway, hesitated, then pushed a wheelbarrow through the oversized opening. "What's going on?"

Mom smiled and walked over to the tarps. "Ron, help me with these. Roberta needs a new place, and this is it. What do you think?"

"I was thinking the same thing." He parked the wheelbarrow under the light. It was heaped with things from the old playhouse: Grandma Benson's old clothes and accessories from the trunk, chipped dishes from the apple crate cupboard, a doll bed Dad had made for me one Christmas.

I pulled the items out of the wheelbarrow one by one, too embarrassed to be as thankful as I should. It felt like something secret, something personal, had been exposed. Grandma had given me the stuff years ago; did Dad wonder why I still wanted it? As I rinsed soot off the dishes in the sink, he helped Mom remove the tarps, revealing a pile of discarded furniture. They picked out a red chrome table and three wobbly, wooden chairs; a faded brown hide-a-bed couch; and a chifforobe. Together we arranged the furniture, but I didn't make eye contact with Dad.

"Well, that about does it." Mom stood near the door, smiling. Dad wheeled the empty barrow toward her.

"Thanks Mom and Dad." I meant the words, even if I couldn't look at Dad as I said them.

They left, but I stayed behind to get the feel of my new place. It smelled musty and dirty. Sawdust spilled from gaps in the wood-slat walls and mouse droppings littered the cracked concrete floor. Shadows swallowed the meager glow from the lone light bulb. It felt nothing like my old playhouse.

I put Grandma's things in the chifforobe. Tomorrow I'd knock down the cobwebs, sweep the floor, and wash the window. Tomorrow it would be better.

A troubling thought surfaced. *I don't really need a playhouse anymore.*

Yes, I do! I argued with myself. *I need a place for make-believe.*

But a nagging doubt lingered. Maybe it was time to grow up and stop hiding behind fantasy games.

Maybe not.

Chapter 3

Mr. Darcy

A WEEK PASSED BEFORE TAMI BROUGHT UP THE STOREROOM. "WHAT do you do out there every night?" she asked as we did the dinner dishes. I couldn't tell if she was making fun of me or really wanted to know.

"Homework or I read or clip coupons from the *Reader's Digest* for Mom." I didn't tell her that I talked to mice and sometimes pretended I was part of an underground railroad for runaway slaves. I didn't tell her that sometimes I played house.

"Isn't it cold?"

"Yeah." I shrugged. "I'm acclimated to it."

"You're *acclimated*? What you are is weird. Bertie, nobody says 'acclimated.'"

I wanted to say, "Jane Eyre does," but I knew she'd just tease me about my reading choices.

When the dishes were done, I went into the living room to get my homework. Dad was watching the CBS Evening News as a reporter spoke in front of the Capitol. "U.S. economic sanctions against Cuba continue. Some sources say more aggressive action is required to combat Cuba's alliance with the Soviet Union. It is feared that Khrushchev plans to place nuclear missiles on Cuban soil . . ."

Dad grumbled something to Mom about "those idiots."

I didn't want to hear it. Not the news nor Dad's griping. I didn't like the words "aggressive action." All of it terrified me. And Dad disagreed with everything President Kennedy did. If the president was wrong, how could our country be right? If our country wasn't right, how could it be safe? I grabbed my homework and dashed outside through the rain to the storeroom. I didn't want to be out there, in the cold by myself, but I couldn't stay in the house.

I flopped on the couch and opened *Uncle Tom's Cabin*, but I couldn't get the words "aggressive action" out of my head. I set the book aside and picked up *Oliver Twist*. I traced the gold-embossed letters on the cover with my finger before putting the book down. I tidied a stack of magazines, scattered them out again; wrote my name in the dust on a chair; wiped it off.

I chose a soft, green dress from the chifforobe and pulled it on over my clothes. The faint smell of smoke reminded me of my old playhouse. I blinked back tears and took off the dress, letting it slip to the floor. *Is the newscast over? Is the living room safe?* My favorite Jane Austen book, *Pride and Prejudice* lay on the edge of the table, a crocheted bookmark sticking out between the pages. *Maybe a gentle game will work, something nonaggressive.* I shimmied into a long, blue dress, the one Grandma said was her favorite, and shoved my feet into the matching high heels.

Elizabeth and Jane Bennett didn't have nuclear bombs to worry about. I sat on a chair and fingered the lacy doily in the middle of the table, wishing I lived a hundred and fifty years ago when no one worried about Communist aggression.

Mice rustled in the shadows. I set the table for tea and when I opened a package of stale soda crackers, a special mouse appeared. "Mr. Darcy," I said with a sophisticated British accent. "Would you care to join me?"

Mr. Darcy, boldest of all the mice, scurried up the chair leg and leaped onto the table. His tail was shorter than other mouse tails and he had a slightly crooked back foot, a result, perhaps, of an encounter with a mouse trap.

"How are you today, sir?" I greeted my guest, expecting him to nibble on the bit of cracker I'd left on a chipped, blue china plate. Instead he darted to the lace doily and chewed on it.

"Hey, Darcy! Eat the cracker, not the doily!"

Mr. Darcy ignored me.

"Put it down," I barked. Suddenly I felt silly dressed in my grandmother's dress with its high ruffled neck and sheer, lacy sleeves, talking to a mouse as if he understood me. I pulled off the dress and stumbled out of the shoes. Glaring at the rodent, I screeched, "Get off my table! Don't touch the doily!"

Mr. Darcy twitched a black-tipped ear and continued nibbling the edge of the lace.

"Go away!"

Stepping toward the table, I tripped over the cast-off shoes and rammed my arm on the table's sharp edge. It didn't bleed, but the pain fed my anger. I picked up the high heel and hurled it at Mr. Darcy. Whoosh! The blow knocked him off the table, onto the wooden chair, then to the concrete floor. He lay motionless, black eyes open.

I pivoted away from the scene and ran smack into a shelf lined with canned peaches. A jar teetered on the edge, then crashed to the floor, spraying my legs with sticky syrup. I raised my arms to cover my head, and my hands hit the dangling light bulb. The light swung back and forth. Shadows swelled and shrank, as if the room were possessed with evil, and the canning jars alive, dancing some weird, witchy dance. I yanked the light's chain and instantly the room turned black. The chain clank-clanked against the bulb as it continued to sway. I swung my arms wildly like tree branches in a windstorm, seeking the chain to bring back the light. In the blackness, I dared not move my feet.

I strained to see. *What is that sound? Is it Mr. Darcy?* As moonbeams filtered through the window, my eyes adjusted to the dark. I bolted barefoot into the rain-soaked night and shoved the door closed behind me. My toes sank in the mud as rain plastered down my hair. Drenched and trembling, I leaned against the door and cried.

Light from the screen porch beckoned me inside. I slogged through the mud, up four wooden steps, and let the screen door bang shut behind me. The washing machine and dryer were silent for now, but rain drummed against the curtainless windows and a low hum came from the freezer. Aaron sat on the high, back ledge of the firewood box, his feet propped on the lower, front ledge. In his left hand he held ropes tied to Palomino Pal, our old rocking horse; in his right hand he gripped a toy pistol.

I scrambled up beside him. Tami saw us through the kitchen window and shook her head. I knew she thought I was too old for such games. Maybe she was right, but right now a pretend game with Aaron was better than the reality of a dead mouse in a cold storeroom—much better than news reports about Cubans and Communists.

Aaron moved over to make room for me; he moved a little more when my wet clothes brushed against him. "Where are we headed?" I asked through chattering teeth.

"Outrunning bandits," he replied grimly. "Got a shipment of gold on board and news of it leaked out. That's Jesse James and his gang back there."

"Give me the reins; I'll drive. You're a better shot."

He handed me the ropes, and fired quick shots off to the side. Bullets whizzed over our heads as we dodged boulders and raced around sharp corners until the last robber was blasted from his horse. This time we survived without broken bones or gunshot wounds; we didn't always. Sometimes our stagecoach transported important people, and we'd be kidnapped and have to outsmart the bad guys to escape. Sometimes outlaws shot us and we'd topple to the ground, where our mortal wounds brought slow, agonizing death. Sometimes the wood box was a chariot and we'd race for our lives like in *Ben Hur*. Tonight's victory made me smile.

Mom called, "Bedtime!" We clambered down and dashed to the door. Halfway through the kitchen, a huge hand grabbed the back of my neck, stopping me in my tracks. Literally. Footprints from my muddy feet sullied the otherwise spotless floor. Dad let go of my neck, turned me around to face him, and gripped my shoulders. Aaron slinked past.

I didn't look up at my father, but I knew he was scowling, and I was afraid, afraid of his scowl, afraid of his intense, gray-blue eyes glaring their disapproval. I couldn't think of what to say and didn't dare move. His thick thumbs dug into my arms. Tears threatened, but crying was sure to annoy him, so I fought against my emotions. *What do I do now? Should I offer to mop up my mess? Wait for him to speak? Apologize? What, what, what! What is the right thing?*

I sniffed before remembering that sniffing riled him as much as crying, but my nose was going to drip if I didn't do something. The drip slid downward. As it bubbled over my nostril, I sniffed again.

The feeble effort came too late and the drip fell onto the muddy floor.

He shook my shoulders slightly in a gesture I knew meant, "Look at me!" As I peered up a tear slipped down, I sniffed. "S-s-sorry."

"What are you bawling about? Looks to me like your mother's the one with a reason to cry—look what you did to this floor!" As he spoke he released my arms. I resisted an urge to rub the sore places, and nodded, signaling that I understood him. He strode away, but returned in seconds with an old towel, and stepped past me. I straggled behind him to the porch steps. He sprayed off the remaining mud from my feet with cold water from the garden hose, and roughly dried them on the towel. On his way back inside he grabbed the mop.

Tami was already asleep, so I wriggled into my nightgown without turning on the light and crawled in bed. There, in the dark, I let the tears flow. Why had I left the warmth of the house tonight? To kill a mouse in a dirty, dingy storeroom? How was that better than listening to war news?

I deserved Dad's scowl, his reprimand. What did I expect him to say? "Hey, Roberta, good job tracking mud on the clean floor."

Dad was mad at me. Make-believe had failed me. And Mr. Darcy was dead.

Chapter 4

Hope

"Minus tides this weekend at Westport," Dad announced at
dinner.

I looked at Mom. It was just the beginning of May, too early for
camping, or was it?

Mom nodded at Dad. "We used the last of the razor clams over a
month ago. I think I can get the camper ready."

Aaron and I smiled at each other. Pacific Ocean, here we come!

By the time Dad got home from work the next day, the *Terry*
camp trailer was scrubbed and packed, ready to go. He hitched the
trailer to our red Chevy station wagon and we all piled in. Mom
leaned her head back against the seat and closed her eyes; she had a
headache. Dad looked at her before turning in his seat to speak to
us. "Play the 'quiet game.'"

That meant no talking. Aaron sat between Tami and me and read
a dinosaur book. I looked out the window as telephone poles stuttered by, and silently pretended I was on a secret mission.

We were fleeing from Communist double agents. Only Dad and
I knew of the danger, but Mom, Tami, and Aaron would be captured unless I decoded the mysterious clues. Dad kept ahead of our

pursuers by skillful driving, but they were closing in. I suspected the headlights of the rusty brown pickup behind us contained special tracking equipment. I activated the anti-tracking shield attached to the back of the camper, but if I didn't solve the code, we would not find the secret entrance to the "Forest of Safety." Mailboxes along the road held the key. As we rolled past, I looked for secret messages in the addresses and names. Just in time I figured out the code and we slipped into the "Forest of Safety" undetected by our enemies. The rusty brown pickup zoomed past the campground entrance.

I scooted out of the car and helped set up camp; we all went to bed early. Nestled in my sleeping bag next to Tami, I thought about Dad. I lived fearful of making him angry. *What if I stop worrying about doing something wrong and just try to do something he'd like?* Usefulness was important to Dad. Maybe tomorrow I could dig clams instead of play. It would show him that I was capable, that I was useful. That was the kind of thing that might please him. I fell asleep determined to impress Dad by digging a limit of clams in the morning.

Dad woke us as the sun was rising. Aaron and I slipped into swimming suits, grabbed our sweatshirts, and climbed into the back of the station wagon. When Mom and Tami were ready, Dad drove to the beach. Drivers often got stuck at the tricky entrance, but not Dad. He sped through the soft ruts, fishtailing slightly, then zipped along the hard-packed sand. The flat beach ran north and south for miles, but Dad always knew the right spot to park, the right place to find the biggest and best razor clams.

As soon as the car stopped, I bolted through the open tailgate window, grabbed one of the short-handled shovels, and skipped toward the ocean. I wanted to be the first to spot the telltale hole signifying a clam beneath the surface. It had to be the right kind of hole, not those made by worms or shrimp or crabs.

Dad shouted above the roaring waves, "Roberta! Watch where you're stepping!"

Oops! I skidded to a stop. I knew razor clams dig for China when they sense the least bit of pressure from above. I knew better than to step on the top of a clam hole. Dad caught up with me and I pointed to a nearby "clam show." I looked up at him.

Here was my chance. If I missed the clam, he would scowl. But if I got it, he would look at me and nod. A nod meant "good job." It was the opposite of a scowl. I would do this useful thing and get a nod.

"Can I?" My voice squeaked.

"May I." Dad corrected my grammar.

"May I?"

"Go ahead."

I placed the narrow, curved blade a few inches to the right of the clam show, the side toward the sea, and quickly dug once and then again, just as I'd seen Dad do hundreds of times. I dropped to my knees and plunged my right hand into the hole I had made. The hole rapidly filled with water. Edges of sand crumbled into the opening. I felt from side to side, and then swiftly scooped out a pile of clean, soggy sand before plunging in again. Quickly, I scraped out another mound of sand and again thrust my hand into the watery hole.

"Come on, Bertie." Aaron dropped to his knees beside me. "Can't ya feel him, yet? Did he get away?"

I scooped and plunged again.

"He got away, huh." Aaron got up and left me.

I dug farther down. There it was! I pinched its neck and tugged steadily until the suction broke. I pulled the clam out of the hole, held it high, and danced in a circle. "I did it! I did it!"

Dad was engaged in his own tug-of-war, his back to me. I stopped dancing. *Should I run over to him? Call to him? Wait for him to finish? How can I get a nod?* I stared at his back. He stood up, took a step, and dug another hole.

An interested seagull eyed my clam as I dropped it in the net pouch dangling from the rope belt around my waist. I ran toward Dad.

He knelt on one knee with his other leg stretched out to the side, one arm swallowed by a hole up to his elbow. I liked the moment the clam first appeared, its "foot" digging in the air as if it were still in the sand. I edged closer but didn't watch where I was stepping. I didn't notice how near I was to Dad's pouch bulging with clams, lying on the sand near his knee. As his arm came up, I clapped my hands and jumped up, then came down on Dad's pouch. Crunch! I hopped back, but the damage was done. I'd smashed maybe a half-dozen clams and cut my foot on the sharp edges of their broken shells.

"Roberta! What's the matter with you?"

I froze, but my brain ran ahead. *Smashed clams! What an idiot!*

"I swear, Roberta! Go on! Get away from the clam beds. For crying out loud, what a mess! And get your hair out of your mouth." Dad's voice was cold, harsh. He didn't say anything about my bleeding foot or the clam in my net pouch. He scowled at the broken shells.

Why did I think I could get a nod? I was not useful. I deserved the scowl. Blood from my cut darkened the sand. I took a deep breath and swallowed hard. *You idiot! Better to stay in the background. Better not to try.* I stared at Dad's back as he continued digging.

"Hey, Bertie, come on!" Aaron's words whisked past in the wind. He ran up to me and grabbed my hand with sandy, cold fingers. "Come on." He pulled me down the beach.

Nearby a creek merged with the ocean. I rinsed my cut in the ankle-deep, icy current. We gathered small pieces of driftwood and threw them in. They bobbed along until they got stuck in the sand.

I waded in the stream and took in the early morning grayness. Thick clouds covered the heavens without a break. The tumbling ocean was as gray as the sky and white-gray foam made peculiar patterns on the dark gray-brown of the wet sand. Dry sand farther away from the water was a softer gray. Sand dollars, driftwood, and broken bits of clamshell dotted the shore, but their drab colors of cream and tan did nothing to brighten the scene. I liked it. People stood out in this neutral background: men in yellow raincoats and red sweatshirts joined children in blue bathing suits and bright orange shorts, like a painting of flittering butterflies on a dull gray backdrop.

I breathed in the salt air and splashed across the stream. Frigid water numbed my feet and ankles. A gust of wind brought goose bumps to my sand-covered legs and arms. Aaron shivered, then put on his sweatshirt.

"I love the wind, Aaron."

"Why?"

"Because it blows radiation away from us."

"What?"

"Never mind." I wished I hadn't said anything. I had not told anyone about my fear of Communists and nuclear war. But right here, right now, I felt safe. If the Soviets launched a nuclear bomb and it landed nearby, the radiation would be blown away. I faced the wind; it ruffled my hair and kissed my cheeks.

I liked everything about the seashore: seagulls crying in the wind, the smell of saltwater and seaweed, chilly waves splashing as high as my knees, sand pulling away from under my feet as the water rushed back to join the other waves. The ocean's rhythmic cycle hypnotized me. The constant roar and ever-changing patterns of unpredict-able, powerful waves thrilled me. The ocean did not make me think about God; it made me feel Him.

I stepped out of the stream and twirled. My pouch with the single clam twirled with me, hitting against my thigh. Dizzy, I fell on the sand, laughing. I hadn't gotten a nod from Dad, he was angry with me again, and my foot hurt. But the ocean was greater than these things. With such a sea, who needed a playhouse for make-believe or a storeroom to hide in?

The ocean was bigger than a nod and more powerful than fear. If I could live by the sea forever, I would be happy.

Chapter 5

Just Do the Job

AFTER OUR LIMITS WERE FILLED AND THE TIDE TURNED, WE returned to camp. While Dad fixed breakfast, I brushed the sand off my arms and legs and dressed in warmer clothes.

Our family had rules. One of them was Work Before Play. We knew that after eating a meal, the dishes would be washed, dried, and put away; that before we left on a camping trip, the house would be set in order; that before we went on a hike, the camp must be tidied.

I never considered what might happen should a dirty dish go unwashed or a bed unmade. The world had a particular order in which things were to be done, and it was my job to follow that order. Mom did not say, "It's time to clean clams," after we ate breakfast. That would have been as ridiculous as saying, "It's time to chew" after taking a bite of food, or "swallow" after drinking.

I took my place in the assembly line. Dad poured boiling water over the clams and scraped them out of their shells into a bowl of cold water. I took a clam from that bowl and, using small, pointed scissors, snipped off the tip of its neck, cut all the way down its length, and then double cut the neck. *One down and a hundred zillion million to go.*

Tami separated the digger from the rest of the clam and made sure the neck and "zipper" were free of sand. Aaron kept the bowls filled with clean water and took away the empty shells. Mom cleaned the diggers. The diggers were shaped a little like a foot. Even though they were separated from the rest of the body, they sometimes squirmed when cut into. It was freaky. Aaron liked it, but I wanted nothing to do with wriggling diggers.

I am useful, I realized as I worked. I'd done this job many times before. Usually I worried about making sure I did it right, but I knew how to do this. There was nothing to worry about.

I looked at my family, working together. Mom and Tami chatted about Cousin Linda's new baby. Dad whistled, "What a Friend We Have in Jesus." Aaron tried to warble along as he emptied murky water from a bowl and refilled it with clean water. The sun peaked through the clouds and warmed my shoulders.

We worked on. After a while my legs throbbed from standing. My wrinkled hands ached from the cold water. I was bored with snipping clam necks, one after another.

I pretended that the people in the next campsite had been captured by a wicked wizard, the mortal enemy of Merlin the Great. The victims were held against their will by an evil spell, but every clam we cleaned weakened the curse. If we did enough clams before the evil wizard returned, the captives would be free to return to Camelot. I snipped as quickly as I could, racing against time to free the tortured souls. The wizard would return at any moment! Snip, Roberta, snip! I clipped faster and faster.

A noisy crow landed on a tree limb. Caw! Caw! A spy for the wizard? I kept my eyes on the black bird as I grabbed a clam from the bowl and snipped, all in one motion. If I had been paying attention, I'd have felt the difference. If I hadn't been caught up in my fantasy,

I'd have realized the thing in my hand did not feel like a clam. But I was watching the crow, not the clams, and I was moving fast.

Aaron yelped and jerked his hand out of my grasp. His index finger dripped blood.

"Roberta!" Dad grabbed Aaron's hand and pinched the wound. Mom rushed into the camper and came back with the first aid kit. Tami snickered.

"I . . . I . . . thought it was a clam."

"You thought your brother's finger was a clam?" Dad glowered as he applied pressure to Aaron's finger tip. "Of all the tomfool things!"

"How bad is it, Ron?" Mom stood ready with a bandage and first aid cream.

I looked away as Dad examined the wound. My stomach churned and the ever-ready tears streamed unchecked. I wanted to say how sorry I was, but the words came out like a hiccough. *How bad is it?* I waited for Dad to answer Mom's question.

"Not bad. Sliced the tip."

"Off? She sliced the tip of my finger off?"

"No, knucklehead. Not off," Dad replied.

I sat beside Aaron on the picnic table bench and put my hand on his shoulder as Dad applied pressure to the wound. Aaron didn't shrug away, but no one spoke to me. Dad's steel-gray eyes silently accused. *Please don't look at me!* One sob escaped, but I held the others back.

"She didn't mean to," Aaron said. "I shouldn't have been playing with the clams. I shouldn't have put my hand in the bowl."

"How can anyone mistake a finger for a clam?" Dad shook his head.

He is right. What kind of idiot mistakes her brother's finger for a clam? What was I thinking? *Stupid make-believe.* Why hadn't I just focused on doing my job?

When the bleeding stopped, Dad bandaged Aaron's wound. Then he picked up the scissors and took over my job. I didn't know what I was supposed to do, so I sat on the bench, watching Mom and Tami and Dad until the rest of the clams were cleaned. It took longer because of the broken shells. And no one whistled or talked.

Chapter 6

Monsters

Sunday, on the way home, we stopped at Grandma Benson's to give her some clams. She lived in a two-story, white house at the end of Lake Saint Clair. We visited her often, but the big house was a mystery to me. I rarely went in the living room and never ventured upstairs. When we visited Grandma Benson, we stayed in her large, cheery kitchen or we played on the docks by the lake.

As we filed in, Grandma nodded toward the cookie jar and Aaron and I raced to see who could get to it first. Tami waited, her eyes measuring Grandma up and down. Grandma laughed. "All right, we can check again, but I doubt you've grown an inch in just a month." Grandma was short—the first adult we knew that we could grow taller than.

They stood back to back and Tami stretched to her full height, but Grandma was still an inch taller. I smiled, pleased that the goal hadn't been reached. I didn't want Tami to be taller than Grandma, even if she was almost fifteen. I wanted her to be a kid, like me.

Tami had faults: she could run faster than I could, climb a tree higher, hit the croquet ball harder, and play the piano jazzier. She had no use for fantasy. And there was another serious flaw: she wasn't afraid of anything. Not even Grandpa Benson.

Grandpa Benson never joined us in the kitchen. Sometimes Dad sat with him in the living room, arguing religion and politics, but mostly we chatted in the kitchen with Grandma and ate her home-made cookies. Grandma stayed alert to Grandpa, but he remained in his big armchair watching television. "Old woman!" he would shout. "I want coffee!"

After Grandma went outside with Mom and Dad to get the clams, Grandpa Benson yelled, "Hey! Bring me my pipe and a match."

Aaron and I stopped chewing our cookies and looked at each other. *If Grandma doesn't respond, will he come into the kitchen for the matches? Will he yell at us?*

Tami nodded as if agreeing to a secret discussion going on in her head. She snatched the matches lying by the stove and calmly walked into the dining room. Aaron and I followed. We crouched by the sideboard.

Tami strode toward Grandpa Benson in the darkened living room, her hand extended with the matches plainly in view. In my mind she was a maiden warrior entering the cave of a fierce dragon.

As she neared his stuffed armchair, she crossed between him and the television. He cursed and threw one of his slippers; it hit her on the head. I stood and gasped, but Tami didn't flee, didn't even flinch. She picked up the slipper, then gave it and the matches to the monster in the chair.

"Where's my pipe?"

"I don't know." Her back straight, her steps unfaltering, she re-turned to the dining room following the same path between Grandpa and the television.

None of us spoke until we were back behind the closed kitchen door. Aaron laughed as he pushed a chair to the middle of the room and sat on it facing the stove. Tami strutted between him and the "television." I giggled.

The adults entered the kitchen just as Aaron cursed and threw a cookie at Tami's head.

I sobered at the look on Dad's face. Tami picked up the cookie from the floor and brashly faced him, but Dad was not looking at her, he was glaring at Aaron. Grandma stood with her hands on her hips. Mom pursed her lips. Dad grabbed Aaron's shirt collar and hauled him outside to Grandpa Benson's woodshed.

Tami shrugged, put the chair back in its place and nibbled on the cookie. I stared at her. Shouldn't she defend Aaron? Explain the situation? It wasn't like it looked. Aaron wasn't really cursing—it was part of the game. Tami's eyes met mine. She shook her head slightly and remained silent. Moments before I had thought my sister the bravest person in the world, now I thought her the most heartless.

Words jumbled around in my head, rammed into each other, and ricocheted back and forth. *Say something, Roberta!* But the words would not line up so that I could get them out of my mouth. A trickle of shame and frustration slid from my eyes. We were all guilty, not just Aaron. It wasn't right that he alone was punished.

On the ride home, I wanted Aaron to know that I was sorry, but the words bounced around in my brain like dropped Ping-Pong balls. I stared out the window while silent tears fell. I hated the way fear controlled me. Fear jumbled words in my head; it pushed me out to the cold storeroom away from the nightly news and my family; it kept me from thinking straight.

At home we unloaded the camper and put things away. After that it was bedtime. I sat on the bottom bunk of the beds Dad had made for Tami and me, thinking about the day instead of putting on my nightgown. I watched Tami lay out her school clothes for the morning. As she bent over, her curls fell forward and she tossed them out of her eyes.

I wished I had her wavy, dark-golden blonde hair instead of my plain, brown mop. My face was round and plump, hers was heart-shaped with high cheekbones. Everything about her was petite and pretty; everything about me was awkward and plain.

Tami wasn't afraid of Grandpa Benson, hadn't even winced when he chucked the slipper at her; didn't yelp when it hit her. Words didn't ricochet in her head like a marble in a pinball machine.

If I were as brave as Tami, I would have stood up for Aaron. What was wrong with her that she didn't try to stop Dad from taking Aaron to the woodshed? I shook my head as her eyes met mine.

"Why are you staring at me?" Tami challenged.

I stood up quickly and grabbed my nightgown. "Wasn't," I mumbled and began to undress. Tami thrust her face forward and stared at me, bug-eyed.

"Stop it," I whined.

"Stop what?"

"Don't watch me get undressed." I knew it was useless. Tami was peeved. She wasn't about to leave me alone tonight.

"Watcha gonna do about it? Cry?"

I sniffed and sat back down on the bed, my nightgown in hand.

Mom came to tuck us in, but I wasn't ready. She waited in the doorway. *Great. Two sets of eyes to avoid*. I twisted the end of my braid. "I don't like to be watched while I get undressed." The words came out louder than I meant.

Rule #2 in our house (right next to Work Before Play) was No Talking Back. Not always sure what talking back was, I stayed careful not to sass at all. My statement sounded sassy to me. Tami and Aaron had been taken to the woodshed for talking back.

Mom came over and sat beside me on the bed, but she didn't say anything, and I didn't know what I was supposed to do. *Do I stay put? Get up and start undressing? Apologize? Wait for her to say something?* The dreaded tears swelled. I sighed.

Mom took my hand and bent her head to look in my eyes. "Take your clothes into the bathroom and change there."

That was it. *Take your clothes into the bathroom and change there.* She said it matter-of-factly. She wasn't angry with me. She wasn't making fun of me. How simple. *Why didn't I think of that?* Nightgown in hand, I wrinkled my nose at Tami, and went into the bathroom to undress.

Chapter 7

Secrets

"WE'RE GOING TO TAKE CARE OF OMA WHEN SHE IS RELEASED FROM the hospital," Dad announced at the dinner table a couple nights after we returned from camping.

I sat up straighter. I didn't know Oma was in the hospital. Why didn't grown-ups tell kids anything?

I knew it was wrong to have favorites, but I loved Oma best of anyone. She was Dad's mom, and everything I wanted in a grandmother. She was round with no sharp edges; even her elbows were dimpled. Her hair was completely white and her face lined and creased, but she was kind and gentle regardless of double chins and thick spectacles. She had false teeth that hurt her gums, so she only put them in to eat. Her shrunken mouth looked comical, but Oma didn't care how she looked; she cared how she loved.

It didn't bother Oma that I still played with dolls. She made clothes for my Barbie and stocked her play cupboard with coloring books, crayons, puzzles, and games. Most importantly, she colored and played the games with us. If Oma had a fault, it was that she couldn't cook. Instead she heated frozen TV dinners and served desserts in the form of Twinkies and Hostess Cupcakes. Aaron liked the cupcakes best.

Preparations were made for Oma to share Tami's room and I moved in with Aaron. My clothes would remain in Tami's closet, and I would still dress and undress in the bathroom. I was jealous that my sister got to room with Oma, but I didn't mind moving in with Aaron. It was a lot better than sharing with Know-It-All Tami.

Dad brought Oma home on Friday while we were at school. When the bus dropped us off, I ran all the way to the house. Mom met me in the kitchen. "Wait, Roberta. She's asleep. Don't disturb her."

Tami and I tiptoed into the room to change from school dresses into play clothes. I didn't want to bother Oma, but I couldn't help touching her arm. Her eyes fluttered opened and she smiled faintly. Her face was gray, her eyes sunken, her lips cracked. From the hallway Dad beckoned us to come away.

He led us into the living room and spoke gravely. "She will ring the bell by her bed if she needs something, otherwise leave her alone; she needs to rest."

Tami blurted out the words I was thinking. "She looks terrible! Will she get better?"

Dad didn't answer, but Mom came in from the kitchen and spoke softly.

"Well, she's advanced in years and she's undergone a serious operation, but the doctor wouldn't have let her come home if he didn't think that was best for her."

I'd been excited about Oma coming to live with us, but I hadn't thought she'd be so sick. I sucked on my braid tip.

I didn't know what to do with myself on such a strange day. Oma was here, but too sick to talk to. Dad was home from work on a weekday. Everyone was speaking in hushed tones and I didn't know the rules for this situation. I hesitated on the porch. *Will I feel better outside?*

Aaron rolled past on his bike, so I got mine out of the toolshed and joined him. I liked the feel of tight leg muscles as I pedaled down the lane and back up again, the wind cold against my face. I passed Aaron and he sped up to overtake me.

We were race car drivers and this was the last lap. The hemlock tree at the top of the hill near the railroad track was the finish line and if I could win this last race, then the silver cup would be mine along with the prize money. I needed the cash so Oma could live in a better climate and recuperate.

Cameras flashed as we neared the checkered flag. We were dead even. I'd need all the skill and power I could muster to pull ahead. I floored the throttle and heard my engine roar. The crowd lining both sides of the race track went crazy. Suddenly another car appeared on the race track, going the wrong way! There wasn't room on the road for three vehicles!

A horn blasted. Tires skidded on gravel.

"Bertie! Stop!"

I steered my bike into the grassy ditch and fell off. Aaron stood astride his bike on the other side of the lane. The car rolled slowly forward and stopped. A white-haired stranger behind the wheel removed his glasses and looked at me. "Well, Well." Pause. "Are you all right?"

"Yes, sir."

"What about that other fellow? Is he okay?"

"Yes, sir." I didn't know if Aaron was okay or not, but all I could think to say was "yes, sir."

"Your grandmother get settled in okay?"

"Yes, sir."

Aaron wheeled his bike around beside me. "You're a doctor."

"Yes, I'm here to check on your grandmother."

"You're not Dr. Bates."

"No. I'm a specialist from Olympia." The doctor paused a minute, looking at both of us as if he wasn't sure it was safe to proceed. Finally he rolled up his window and continued toward the house.

"Bertie, didn't you see him? You almost rode right into his car! What were you thinking?"

"I wanted the prize money for Oma."

"What prize money?" Without waiting for an answer, Aaron pedaled his bike home. I followed slowly.

Aaron had a problem I hadn't known about until I shared his room: he wet the bed. Sometime before dawn, he would change his underwear, steal one of my blankets, and curl up on the braided rug by my bed. I wasn't always aware that he was there until I stepped on him when I got up. I didn't say anything to him; it was something we did not talk about. Night after night he slept on the floor; morning after morning, he stripped the sheets off his bed and put them in the washing machine, as routine as the rooster crowing in the morning, as common as rain in spring.

Aaron had great toys even if they were for boys, especially his Tonka trucks. The dump truck, grader, and crane were a solid construction yellow; the tractor and plow were a bright green, and the hook-and-ladder fire engine a shiny crimson. Aaron and I bargained over our toys. We agreed that if I played trucks with him, he'd play Barbie dolls with me. After we made our deal, we never mentioned it again, and we never discussed where we would play. We played with the trucks outside on a graveled lane by the garage. We played Barbies in our room with the door shut.

The secrets I knew about Aaron—that he wet the bed and that he played with dolls—made me feel close to him. I was never tempted to tell them to Tami. I did tell Oma. I wasn't tongue-tied with her.

Confined to her bed, Oma welcomed our visits. Aaron played marbles on the floor in her room or drew pictures for her and taped them to the walls. Tami read to her from the Bible or sang hymns in her soft, clear voice.

After school or when the dishes were done, I sat on the edge of Oma's bed or lay down beside her and told her anything that popped into my head. I loved that she was lying in bed, not doing laundry, or sweeping the porch, or sewing, or weeding the garden—tasks that claimed Mom's attention. When I sat down to talk to Oma, the only distraction was when she fell asleep.

Ten days passed without me once fleeing to the storeroom. I escaped the evening news and Dad's scowl by talking to Oma or doing my homework by her bedside. Commies, Cubans, and the woodshed lost their power over me when I was snuggled next to Oma.

One day after school I plopped myself on the corner of her bed and jostled her awake. When we had gotten off the school bus, Tami had thrown a rock in a puddle spattering my school dress with muddy water.

"Come and get me, Baby-Bertie," she taunted as she skipped away.

Tears trickled and I sniffed as I told Oma about it. I expected her to sympathize with me, to criticize Tami for being mean.

She listened with her eyes closed. When I stopped talking, she opened them and looked wearily at me. She put her hand on my arm and spoke in a thin, cobwebby voice, "You're a lot purtier when ya ain't crying." Then she closed her eyes again.

"How do I stop crying?" I whispered to her sleeping form. "Tell me, Oma. How do I fight tears? How do I stop being afraid?"

The next day Mom intervened as I headed back to Oma's room after school. "Don't talk to her right now, Roberta. She needs to sleep."

I tiptoed through her door to get my play clothes. Oma had been with us for two weeks, but she looked worse than when she first came. Her face was ashen, her eyes sunken, her breathing labored.

I changed my clothes and found Mom in the kitchen. "Mom? Oma looks . . ."

"I know. I called the doctor. He's coming as soon as he can."

I put on a sweater and fled to my secret garden. The garden was a shady spot partway down a knoll and protected from the wind. In the spring, two colossal dogwood trees made a canopy over newly sprouted ferns and delicate trilliums. I liked sitting on the mossy ground, dreaming fantasies where I always did and said the right things. I couldn't go to my garden after dark or in the rain, but I went as often as weather and daylight permitted.

I was there the day Aaron set fire to my playhouse. I returned now to think about Oma. I imagined she and I were sailing with Jim Hawkins and Long John Silver on a boisterous sea. I climbed a tall mast and waved to her below. The wind whipped my hair and the sea slapped a salty mist on my face. I spied the skull and cross-bones of a pirate ship, but we outwitted the scalawags and made off with their treasure on our way to France where Oma was going to take cooking lessons. I wasn't afraid of the height of the crow's nest. I didn't get nauseous on the rolling ocean swells. I didn't wonder what to do next, or what terrible thing might happen; whatever I did was the right thing to do and I could handle anything.

Raindrops spattering through the trees aroused me, but before I reached home the sprinkles became a cloudburst. As I ran, I saw Aaron dashing ahead of me. We arrived on the screen porch, both soaking wet. Mom decided a hot bath would help ward off sniffles, and that's when I joined my sister in playing a mean trick on my brother. Most of my blunders were accidents; I did this stupid thing on purpose.

Chapter 8

Tears

AFTER I FINISHED MY BATH, AARON WENT IN TO TAKE HIS. "HEY, Bertie, come here," Tami motioned me into the bedroom where Oma lay snoring softly. I knew we shouldn't be in there; Mom said not to disturb her until after the doctor came.

Tami touched my elbow and whispered. "Since you're sharing Aaron's room now, you can go in there whenever you want, right? Well, you should go in now, but just stand in the doorway while I stand here."

Tami including me in a plan? The bathroom door was in the middle of the hallway. Our bedrooms were at opposite ends with the doorways facing each other. After a bath, Aaron always darted, naked, from the bathroom to his bedroom; it was only about three steps. I don't know why he didn't take clothes with him or wrap himself in a towel, but he never did.

Standing in his doorway was a mean trick to play on my brother, but how could I refuse Tami? She never included me in anything. I didn't consider whether or not it was the right thing to do, or who might get hurt. I didn't think about how shameful the prank was.

Tami and I waited and when we heard the water draining from the tub, we took our positions, she in her doorway and I in Aaron's.

The bathroom door opened, and Aaron dashed toward his room, only there I was blocking the way. He turned to run back, and there stood Tami, laughing silently and pointing at him. He tore back into the bathroom and slammed the door.

"Mom!" he yelled. "Mom!"

Mom rushed to the hallway. "Aaron!" she scolded through the closed door. "Hush! Your poor grandmother!"

Oma! Tami was offering her a drink of water, talking softly and looking as innocent as a Red Cross worker. Oma needed her rest; all that noise had to have upset her. What a stupid thing to do!

Aaron came out of the bathroom wrapped in a towel. He nudged past me without saying a word. I felt ugly and wicked inside, but I didn't tell him I was sorry. The good feeling I had about doing something with Tami was squashed by the bad feeling of not having done the right thing. I wanted to say something, to at least tell Mom that disturbing Oma wasn't Aaron's fault, but the words leap-frogged in my head. They never made it out my mouth.

Oma would understand. Talking to her would squelch the ugliness I felt. Before my playhouse burned, I never tricked my brother, I was never mean to him. *What is wrong with me?* Tami and Aaron got into mischief regularly, but I constantly tried to do the right thing. I didn't always escape Dad's scowl, but I avoided the woodshed by obeying the rules.

I decided to tell Oma about it after the doctor left, so I sat on my bed and waited for him. Through my opened bedroom door, I could see her sleeping, her face calm and peaceful. Her snoring had stopped. She lay motionless. *She's asleep again. When she wakes up, I can talk to her.*

Dad came home before the doctor got there and went into her room. He touched her arm. "Mother. Mother." Then he groaned, "Oh, no."

He put his fingers on her wrist, then on her neck. He bent closer, placing his ear close to her face. "Mother!"

He shoved aside her pillow, tipped her head back and put his mouth over hers. He pushed on her chest with both hands and yelled, "Help! Help!"

He couldn't see me in the shadows of my room, but I knew I should do something. *Run, Roberta! Get Mom!* My brain barked orders, but I sat huddled on my bed, chewing the tip of my braid.

Mom entered the hallway, a kitchen mitt still on one hand. She stopped in the doorway. I heard Dad's voice but did not grasp his words. Mom rushed away.

Dad kept working on Oma, back and forth from head to chest. When Mom returned she touched his arm. "The ambulance is on its way." Mom took over pushing on Oma's chest, stopping after so many pushes for Dad to breathe into her mouth.

The ambulance and the doctor arrived at the same time crowding the little hallway with people and equipment. I stayed on my bed, silently staring at the activity as if it were unreal, as if it were not happening here and now.

Dad and Mom moved back as the doctor took over. He examined Oma, then turned to Dad. "I'm sorry. It's too late."

Dad knelt by the bed and laid his head on Oma's chest. He put his arms over her. His shoulders trembled slightly, and then harder. Soon his body convulsed with silent heaves. Mom stood beside him and rubbed his back, but he didn't seem to notice.

Dad never cried. He was strong, like Uncle Dan's big bull. Sometimes I trembled before his strength, but I depended on it, too.

Dad is crying. Is Oma okay? Of course not. Dad is crying. How could so much change in so short a time? One minute I was waiting to tell Oma how terrible I felt, and the next everything was topsy-turvy.

I didn't notice Aaron on the floor in the shadows until he got up. He wore his Little League uniform and held a ball in his mitt. We sat together on his bed with our backs against the wall where we could not see what was going on. Neither of us spoke. Aaron tossed his ball up and caught it in his glove over and over. It made a soft plunk as it hit the worn leather.

The room grew darker, but I didn't want to turn on the light. The white baseball floated dimly in the dusky room, up and down, up and down. Plunk, plunk, plunk. Tears streamed, but my mind was still. It was as if a thick, black curtain had silenced everything but the plunk of the baseball.

A nervous energy swelled inside me. My senses flashed from numb to nervous. I scooted off the bed and didn't stop walking until I was in the storeroom. A cloud of dust puffed up when I plopped on the couch. I sneezed.

I remembered Oma's words when Tami splashed muddy water on my dress. She said I was prettier when I didn't cry, but I didn't care about being pretty right now. I wanted Oma back. I wanted Dad strong. I cried out loud. My cries turned to wails. No one could hear me; there was no reason to hold back. I hit my fists on the couch and on my legs. I shook my head and stomped my feet. The wails swelled until my throat grew hoarse, but still I blubbered. I don't know when I fell asleep.

I opened my eyes to the glare of a flashlight and a rough hand shaking me. "I swear, Roberta, with everything else going on, can't you use some sense?" Dad grasped my arm and helped me off the couch. "Get in the house."

Mom's sister, Auntie Marge sat at the kitchen table drinking coffee, an opened Bible in her lap. She reached out to hug me as I walked past, her fingers warm against my cold skin. "Roberta, how long you been out there without a coat? You've got the sense of a gnat."

Mom sighed, rose from her chair and gently touched my face. "You need to warm up. A hot bath will do it. Come on."

I was too old for Mom to run my bathwater, but I followed her as if I were a toddler unable to think or act for myself. I sat in the warm tub as words echoed in my mind. *Oma is gone. Dad cried. I have the sense of a gnat.*

It wasn't until I touched my damp towel that I realized this was my second bath in the space of a few hours.

Chapter 9

*D*iscoveries

WHEN I WOKE IN THE MORNING, I KNEW SOMETHING WAS WRONG, but my mind was foggy. As the haze lifted, sadness settled in my heart.

I stepped over Aaron, shoved my feet into slippers, and entered the hallway. The door to Tami's room was shut, the house quiet. I tiptoed through the dining room, into the kitchen. Mom and Tami sat at the table, a coffee mug in front of Mom, hot chocolate for Tami. Tami had been talking in her soft, clear, Bible-reading voice, but stopped when I came in. Both of them had red, swollen eyes. A crumpled handkerchief lay on the table; Mom held another one in her hand. I felt like an intruder, as if I had interrupted a secret meeting. I mumbled, "Good morning."

"Good morning," Mom muttered back.

I didn't know what else to say, and an awkward silence fell over the three of us.

I shuffled out of the kitchen and back to the hallway. I started to open the door to Tami's room to get my clothes, but stopped. *Is Oma still there? Is she lying dead in the bedroom? Is that why the door is closed?* I loved my grandmother and had never been afraid of her, but I couldn't open the door. I couldn't go into the room.

I knew about death from books. In the books a dead person was put on a table or something in the parlor, and people walked past to say their goodbyes. We didn't have a parlor; would they leave her in the bedroom? Bring her out to the living room? I ached that I hadn't said goodbye, that I hadn't told her I was sorry for disturbing her sleep. But I couldn't talk to a dead body. I slipped back to the living room and sat on the sofa.

Tami came in. "You better get dressed. People will start coming soon, and there is work to do."

What people? Why? To walk past Oma and say their goodbyes? Already?

"Am I supposed to wear black? I don't have black."

"No, Bertie. You don't wear black. Just get dressed, unless you want everyone to see you in your nightgown."

"But, I can't go in there." Tears ran freely.

"Oh, brother!" Tami stomped out of the living room but returned shortly with my clothes. She tossed them at me and they fell scattered on the living room rug. I grabbed them up, scooted into the bathroom, and dressed. When I entered the kitchen again, Mom was talking on the phone and Tami was making more coffee. Aaron sat at the table eating toast and canned peaches. I gulped a glass of milk and went out to the storeroom.

I couldn't think of Oma as dead. I couldn't think at all, and the storeroom felt dingy and cold, a poor substitute for a warm grandmother. I left it and wandered out to my garden. The morning sun thinned the damp fog, but the ground was too wet to sit on. I ambled deeper into the small forest, no destination in mind, no hurry to get anywhere. I watched a trail of ants on a tree trunk, then took a stick and poked a spider web. The spider came out from hiding when the web wiggled. *Sorry, Charlotte. It's a stick, not your lunch.*

The sun won its battle with the fog and rays filtering through the trees made interesting shapes with shadow and light. The rat-a-tat-tat of a woodpecker caught my attention and I looked up through the boughs to find him. A slight breeze softly swayed the tree limbs. I was soothed by the peacefulness of the forest, the caressing movement of the trees rocking slowly back and forth, waving their branches in friendly, graceful gestures. The air smelled damp, but freshly scented with fir and cedar. I lifted my hands above my head, stretched on tiptoes, and swayed as if I too were a mighty tree bending with the wind.

I sauntered down a gentle slope. At the bottom the ground was spongy, in places swampy. I stepped on bracken ferns and salal with my bare feet trying to find the firmest ground for safer walking. When the brush gave out, I slipped from tree to tree, struggling to keep my balance. Gooey mud squished between my toes as if I were walking through half-melted ice cream.

The dank air reeked of rotting wood, stagnant water, and foul skunk cabbage. Pesky gnats swarmed around my face; hungry mosquitoes feasted on my arms. I zigzagged through the marsh, trying not to think about Oma in the bedroom or Dad crying over her. I tried so hard not to think about them that I did not pay attention to where I was going until I almost stepped on Aaron.

"Would ya watch where you're going!"

He climbed up on a giant boulder and dug with a stick at the lichens that covered it. I clambered up on the rock and sat beside him, with my back to his side.

Was this his special place, the place where he escaped when he needed to be alone? I didn't want to intrude, but I didn't want to be alone anymore either. I sat on the mossy rock listening to the breeze share secrets with the trees.

"Hey, what's that?" Aaron jumped down from the boulder and jogged to something poking up out of the mud.

When he hit it with his stick, it didn't sound like a rock, but the part that showed was too white to be wood.

I inched down from the boulder and stood beside him. "Dig it up."

"Help me."

I searched for something to use as a digging tool and found a fallen limb, but it was rotten and broke into pieces when I stuck it in the mud. Aaron worked away the muck from the mysterious object with his stick and his hands. It looked like a bone. I stared at it, wondering how it got in our swamp.

Aaron picked it up. It was a huge skull and jawbone. Our eyes met and my brother licked his lips. He spoke in a hushed, low voice, "A dinosaur."

"Yeah. Wow. A dinosaur."

The triangle rang, calling us home. We hid the bone behind the boulder and covered it with fallen branches. We didn't say, "Don't tell; let's keep this our secret." We knew it was our secret. What a secret!

"There are more bones. We'll come back and find them." Aaron spoke excitedly as we traipsed home. "We'll get shovels and dig up lots more." We did not return the way I had come, but made a big circle coming in behind the house near the storeroom.

"We could bring the pieces here and assemble it." I nodded toward the storeroom. It was his discovery and I didn't want to take it over, but the storeroom would be the perfect place to conceal the mystery until we chose to reveal it to the world.

"It's a dinosaur," Aaron repeated.

"Yeah. What kind, do ya think?"

"Maybe one that hasn't been named yet." His blue eyes glistened. "We'll put the bones together in your playhouse, and we'll go to the library and find out what kind it is."

He paused. Then he murmured, more to himself than to me, "Dad is gonna be proud." And I knew another secret about my brother.

Chapter 10

Cold

Cars and trucks cluttered our lane; some parked on the lawn. When we entered the kitchen, the sorrow in the house squelched my excitement like a bullfrog zapping a fly. Tami grabbed my arm and pulled me close. She whispered, "Go sit by Aunt Ella. She's driving me crazy."

"Who is Aunt Ella?"

A short, round woman burst through the dining room door. "Tamara Thorne, have you no regard for a suffering woman's nerves? Where is my tea? With all I'm going through is a little tea too much to ask? Is this how you took care of . . ." She stopped her tirade when she saw me.

"You must be Roberta."

"Yes, ma'am." *Is this the woman Tami wants me to sit with?*

"You don't look anything like a Thorne."

"She looks like her mother." I hadn't noticed Auntie Marge when I first came in, but she stood beside me now, drying her hands on a dishtowel. Something in her tone of voice hinted that Aunt Ella was not her favorite person.

Aunt Ella frowned at my bare feet and smudgy jeans. "You been playing outside like this is any old day? Don't you care a smidgen about your grandmother, my mother?" Her voice screeched higher with each syllable.

Auntie Marge whisked between the weeping woman and me. She hooked her arm around Aunt Ella's elbow and turned her around. "Sit down, Ella, and drink your tea." Auntie Marge escorted her back through the swinging door. Tami followed, a steaming, rose teacup in hand.

Guilt attacked my heart as I realized that I'd forgotten about Oma when we found the bone. That fast. *What is wrong with me?* Well, I was thinking about her now. I ached to plop on her bed and tell her about our dinosaur. I wanted to snuggle up against her, even if she did fall asleep. Oma had been a barrier between me and news reports about Commies and war. She had been a shield protecting me from Dad's scowl and the woodshed. She'd been an eager listener to my successes and joys.

Why wasn't Dad like her? I wanted to crawl on my daddy's lap, like I could cuddle with Oma. I wanted him to stroke my hair and tell me everything was going to be all right. But I didn't know how to make that happen, and Oma wasn't here to tell me. I wished I had asked her how to talk to my dad. But now she was gone, and I couldn't ever ask her anything again.

Aunt Ella and other family members from California stayed with us, so Tami, Aaron, and I slept in sleeping bags in the living room. The California relatives were strangers to me. They lived too far away for common visiting and Dad didn't talk about them. Aunt Ella unnerved me with her constant whining and complaining.

On the second night of sleeping in the living room, sounds from the kitchen woke me. Aunt Ella's voice rumbled loud and angry. Her words came out in such a rush, I couldn't understand most of them, but there was no mistaking her rage. She was talking about Oma's death. I heard "God Almighty" and "not fair" and "pointless." Then she spoke slowly, as if pausing between each word would give it more meaning. "Why did God allow this to happen to me?"

A chair scooted on the linoleum. Dad's voice sounded controlled and strong. "Ella, I don't suppose any of us are so good as to deserve the blessings we receive. Bad and good things happen to all people. I don't understand it, but I trust God."

I crawled back in my sleeping bag. I hadn't thought about Oma's dying as either a good or bad thing, just a sad thing. *Did God cause Oma's death?* I didn't know much about God, only some Bible stories about people like Moses and Noah because we went to Sunday school and church. Dad said grace before our meals, but that was just something we did; I didn't think it meant anything.

The day of the funeral was overcast and drizzly. Aunt Ella complained how cold it was, but this was May. Why would it be warm? Summer doesn't come to the Northwest until after the Fourth of July.

The wet grass soaked my shoes as we walked from the car to the burial site. A large white canopy covered a seating area and beautiful sprays of flowers surrounded the casket. I knew Oma's body was in it and I didn't want to know that. I didn't want to see a box, no matter how ornately carved, and think about my grandmother shut in it. And one more thing. I didn't want to see Dad cry again. It frightened me more than his scowl. I stood near the casket, next to Dad, a strand of hair in my mouth, trembling.

"Roberta, be still." Dad spoke just loud enough for me to hear, but I couldn't stop quavering. He whispered something to Mom.

"Roberta, come with me." I followed Mom to the back of the crowd where Auntie Marge stood with Uncle Dan.

Mom's face appeared calm. Her eyes were watery, not overflowing with tears, just moist. I looked around at the people, some stoic, some crying softly, some like Aunt Ella, wailing noisily.

I didn't know how to feel. I loved Oma and now she was gone. *Can she see me from heaven?* I looked up. The dark clouds parted and the sun's rays lit up the top layer of a puffy cumulus cloud, transforming the gray into bright white. Sunrays streamed through the hole in the clouds like a waterfall of sunshine. Mom saw it too through moist eyes and smiled. "See," she whispered to me, "all heaven is welcoming Oma home."

Then I felt like crying, like joining the others who were weeping noisily, but I didn't. I choked back the sobs. I held back the tears. Oma thought I was prettier that way.

Chapter 11

Just Plain Silliness

BETWEEN OMA'S DEATH AND OUR SCHOOL WORK, AARON AND I HAD
been unable to return to the marsh. But the last day of school finally
arrived and the entire summer waited. An early dismissal meant
Tami, Aaron, and I rode home on the same bus. It dropped us off
where our lane met the highway.

We skipped the quarter mile, swinging our book bags and singing:

> Row, row, row your boat
> Gently down the stream,
> Push your teacher overboard
> And listen to her scream!

We chanted: "No more school, no more books. No more teachers' dirty looks!"

Aaron taught us a new song to the tune of "The Battle Hymn of
the Republic." We belted it out at the top of our lungs:

> Our eyes have seen the glory of the burning of the school.
> We have tortured all the teachers; we have broken every rule.

The boys are playing poker, and the girls are shooting pool.
As the school burns on and on.
Glory, glory, hallelujah!
Teacher hit me with a ruler.
I bopped her on the bean with a rotten tangerine,
And she won't bother me no more!

We marched up the steps, through the screen porch and into the kitchen, still singing.

"Stop! That song is absolutely sacrilegious! Stop it, right now." Mom's eyes swept from me to Tami to Aaron. She set the plate of cookies she was holding on the counter and glared at us.

Instantly I was deflated. *It's just a song about the last day of school,* I thought, then lowered my eyes to hide my insolence. Mom was angry and I had something to do with it; those facts had always been enough to bring me to tears. What had come over me? Instead of remorse, I felt annoyed at Mom for stopping our fun.

Mom stood with her hands on her hips, frowning. She focused on Tami. "You should know better. I ought to wash your mouth out with soap."

Tami swaggered over to the kitchen sink, picked up a bar of Lava and then, eyes locked defiantly on Mom, she bit the soap.

Mom sank into a chair. Aaron fidgeted. Worried he would do something rash, I put my hand on his arm. It was delay enough, for at just that moment, Mom's smile returned. She shook her head, slowly, pensively, and then chuckled lightly. She looked at Tami and shook her head again. Tami opened her mouth and tiny bubbles escaped. Mom's chuckles rippled and the ripples erupted into guffaws.

I didn't know what was so funny. Mom wouldn't laugh at a sacrilegious song or Tami's impertinence, would she? In spite of my confusion, I giggled. I didn't know why I was laughing, but it didn't matter. Aaron and I held our sides as we hooted and pranced about. Still chuckling, Mom took a cookie from the plate, handed it to Tami, and poured her a glass of milk. They hugged and Tami joined our laughing until our eyes watered and our stomachs hurt.

At dinner, we handed Dad the sealed, manila envelopes enclosing our report cards. They were addressed to "Mr. and Mrs. Ronald Thorne," and Dad reserved the right to open them. I had put the envelope in my book bag as soon as Mrs. Griffin handed it to me, so I wouldn't be tempted to peek. The kids on the school bus opened theirs and either quickly hid them again, or bragged about their grades.

It was hard not to participate. I always received good grades, but never got to boast. At least I would earn approval from Dad; high marks were rewarded with a nod at the dinner table. A nod in front of the whole family.

Dad opened Aaron's card first and took his time examining it. When he looked up, he met Aaron's eyes and nodded. He handed the card to Mom. "Well, it's not perfect. Got some work to do on penmanship."

Mom looked at the report and beamed. I smiled at Aaron, glad he was given slack for less than perfect penmanship. It was my turn next. Dad held the envelope in his hands and frowned. "This is already opened. Roberta, did you open it?"

Did I open it? No! Of course not! I shook my head.

Dad looked at me, then back at the envelope. "Was it sealed when Mrs. Griffin gave it to you?"

I tried to remember. Mrs. Griffin had handed it to me and I put it in my book bag. I didn't know if it was sealed or not. I just didn't know.

"It's a simple question, Roberta. Did you open this envelope addressed to me?"

My eyes filled with water as my head filled with words. I looked down at my plate so he wouldn't see my tears, and shook my head.

"Can't hear your head rattle. Answer me."

I didn't know whether or not the envelope was sealed, but I did know that I had not opened it. *Why can't I just say that?* My throat was tight, dry. "No," I squeaked out the one word. I should have said, "No, sir. I did not open the envelope," but the words wouldn't come.

What if he doesn't believe me and takes me to the woodshed for lying? But I'm not lying!

I wiped my drippy nose on a napkin and waited. It was going to be all right. I breathed deeply, calming myself. Dad would look at the report card and be pleased. It was starting out all wrong, but it would end okay. I sat expectantly, forcing my breath to come slow and even.

Dad put down my envelope and picked up Tami's. "Well, Tamara, let's see how you did."

I felt as if I'd been punched in the stomach. *No! I'm supposed to get a nod.* Four times a year we get report cards. That's four nods. *Dad, don't pass over me!*

Without asking to be excused, I ran from the table. Crying loudly, I stumbled through the screen porch, down the stairs, past the woodshed, and into the storeroom. I flung myself on the couch and wailed. I half-expected Dad to follow and haul me back. Before long, Mom came. She sat down beside me on the couch.

"That was a little silly, don't you think?"

"I didn't open the envelope, Mom. I put it in my book bag as soon as I got it. I wanted to open it, but I didn't."

"So why didn't you say that? We believe what you say."

I didn't answer. How could I explain how my brain turned to mush when faced with Dad's scowl? I didn't understand it; how could I expect anyone else to? I *was* silly.

"Well, there are dishes to do, so come on. You can't hide out here."

She was right. This was no place to hide.

Chapter 12

Digging for Bones

My silliness in running away in tears provided plenty of ammunition for Tami to make fun of me as she washed the dishes and I dried them, but minutes passed and she didn't say anything. *Why isn't she teasing me? What is she thinking?* When she finished washing the last pan, she went into the living room. Curious, I followed.

Flickering light from the television blended with the soft glow of the floor lamp. I glanced at the TV. A weatherman stood in front of a map forecasting sun breaks. Mom rocked in Oma's old, wooden chair knitting a sweater, and counting stitches under her breath. Dad relaxed in his easy chair reading the newspaper. Tami stood in front of him. She waited a moment. When he didn't acknowledge her, she cleared her throat noisily.

"Dad."

He looked up from the paper. "Yes."

"I need you to do something for me. I've given it a lot of thought and I've decided I want to be a writer. I want to write a play this summer, but I need privacy and time to focus on it, so I want to live in the camper until I'm finished. I want to work without interruptions and see what I can do."

Dad folded the paper in his lap. He looked at her for a full minute before answering. I held my breath. What would he say? I watched Tami's face for a clue to what she was feeling. She looked at ease, unworried. Not a hint of nervousness anywhere.

"Where would you like the camper parked?"

Huh? He's going along with it?

"Under the apple tree."

"When?"

"Would this weekend be all right?"

Dad rubbed his chin.

Mom looked from Tami to Dad, her needles resting in her lap. "You'll join us for meals, of course."

"I'd rather not. Couldn't I just fix my own in the camper? I'll keep it clean and take care of it. I really want to be alone as much as possible. It's important to me."

Dad looked as though he was ready to grant her request, but Mom appeared doubtful. "I don't know. What if we decide to go camping?"

"I'll keep it really clean, Mom. It won't take any longer to get it ready for a camping trip. I won't do anything to mess it up."

Mom spoke to Dad. "You think it's okay?" He nodded.

"Far be it from me to stand in the way of your career." She smiled as she picked up the knitting from her lap and recounted the stitches.

Why were things so easy for Tami? Even if I wanted to live alone in the camper, I'd never muster enough nerve to ask.

Sunday after church I watched Dad park the trailer under the apple tree.

Tami opened its door, but didn't step inside. "Oh, no. Dad, you gotta see this."

He looked over her shoulder. "Get a broom and mop. Tell Mom

you need some disinfectant." I looked inside after they left. Mouse droppings speckled the floor.

After Tami swept and mopped, Dad returned with a gallon jar full of what looked like oatmeal, but I knew better. The oatmeal was laced with rat poison. He put an old, plastic, coffee container lid under the camper sink and poured the poison in it. Then he handed me a dozen or so lids. "Follow me, Roberta." He headed into the house.

I put the lids where he directed, and he filled them with poison: under the kitchen sink; behind the washing machine, water heater, sewing machine, and gas stove; on the back, lower shelf in the pantry; in the back of closets; and even a few in the storeroom. It didn't take long to empty the gallon jar. "Go wash your hands," was all Dad said when we were done.

Poor, poor mice. After washing my hands, I grabbed *The Adventures of Doctor Dolittle* from the bookshelf and spent the rest of the afternoon in my secret garden wishing I could talk—really talk— to the animals. I would warn the mice to stay out of the house, out of the camper. No matter how hard I tried I couldn't imagine away the poisoned oatmeal. Maybe mice didn't like oatmeal. Maybe they wouldn't eat it.

Monday morning Aaron and I prepared to explore the marsh and dig out the dinosaur bones. I packed a lunch for us and filled a canteen with water. Aaron carried the shovels he'd pilfered from Dad's toolshed. Mom was working in the flower beds near the camper when we crept out of sight.

We were the leading members of a top-secret excavation team and Aaron was in command. "You keep watch; I'll dig," Aaron ordered. Secrecy was paramount, so I climbed to the top of the boulder and stood, rotating slowly, keeping watch in all directions.

The car-sized boulder was flat on top although it jutted up out of the ground at an awkward angle. Trees towered above, blocking much of the sky, while dense underbrush provided perfect hiding places for spies to lurk. The mosquitoes had been annoying when we found the first bone, but now there were more of them. I stood on the rock, revolving like the second hand of a clock in slow motion, and swatting insatiable mosquitoes that bit my hands, face, and back. I slapped my arm and killed one, but two more took its place.

How was Aaron doing? I looked down. He was bent over, his back to me, digging away, apparently unaffected by the hungry pests.

"Hey, boss," I called to him. Slap! *One down, a zillion to go.*

The boss faced me. I gasped. His head, arms, and hands were smeared with mud. Thick, dark smudges coated his face; his blond hair appeared black. "Read it in a book," he explained. "It's working so far."

I climbed down from the boulder, ready to try anything to lessen the mosquito attack. I didn't roll up my sleeves, but smeared mud over the fabric. Aaron helped me get my face, neck, and back coated as well and then I plastered mud on his back. We looked at each other and I grinned, but bits of mud fell in my mouth, tasting like sewer sludge. I spat. We stank as if we'd been rolling in skunk cabbage.

I pretended the mud was a potent magic, like Bilbo's ring, that made me invisible. Before climbing back on the rock, I gathered a pocketful of stones to use as weapons against potential enemies. I took aim at a clump of underbrush and threw a rock in the midst of it.

"Spies everywhere!" I called down to the leader of our top-secret mission. "I'll keep them away with grenades." I launched rock after rock into the underbrush all around us. "Ka-Pow! Ka-Pow!" I yelled as each grenade hit its target.

"Shut up."

"What?" I had heard him; I just didn't know why he said it. We weren't allowed to say, "Shut up," so I knew he was peeved.

He leaned on the shovel and motioned me to come to him.

"This isn't make-believe," he said as I approached. "We found a real dinosaur bone and we're going to find more. Just stop with the pretending."

All at once, we weren't secret members of an excavation team anymore. We were just two kids, playing in the mud—with buried bones. Only we weren't playing because it was real; we didn't need make-believe. I stayed in the marsh and helped Aaron dig. My back complained from the constant stooping, my arms and shoulders ached from lifting the shovel again and again, and my stomach growled with hunger. We couldn't hold our sandwiches with mud-covered hands, nor could we eat with mud-covered faces, so we plowed on.

Our hands blistered. The blisters stung when they broke open, and smarted more when the mud encrusted them. I couldn't straighten out my aching fingers and grime caked under my fingernails. Still, we didn't give up. We searched through every inch of the bog. We found no more bones.

Aaron took off his shirt and wrapped it around the skull bone. A fresh onslaught of mosquitoes attacked his bare skin. I swatted them off and we raced up the hill. Back among the trees, Aaron poked me with his bundle.

"We found one bone."

"Yeah, we found one bone," I mumbled dejectedly.

"Well, it's a bone. We found it. It's still an amazing discovery."

"And it's still our secret."

We took the amazing discovery into the storeroom and placed it on the table. Aaron ran his fingers along the teeth. "See these?"

"Yeah."

"This wasn't a meat-eater; these teeth are for grinding, not tearing. That's why it was in the swamp. It probably had lots and lots of vegetation once and it lived there and ate all it wanted."

"How do you know so much about dinosaurs?"

"Read about them, and our teacher taught us some stuff."

We looked at the skull and jawbone lying on the table until we were chilled clear through. Aaron covered the bone with an old tablecloth. As he started to put his shirt back on, I realized our clothes were ruined. We weren't ready to make our find public, so we couldn't explain to Mom why our clothes were caked with mud. We'd be forgiven when she realized the importance of our valuable discovery, but we weren't ready to share our secret.

We helped each other wash in the little sink below the window, but there was no soap or hot water. Aaron rinsed out his shirt to use as a washcloth, but it just smeared the slime around on our faces and arms. I dunked Aaron's head under the faucet to wash the mud out of his hair; he did the same for me. The cold water rinsed out the largest chunks, but mostly it gave me a headache. It did not remove the stench.

How were we going to get back in the house? We couldn't put our shirts back on and our jeans were just as bad. I had an idea.

"Aaron, take off your pants. We'll leave our clothes here and put on my dress-up clothes to get back to the house." I took the blue and green dresses from the chifforobe.

"I'm not wearing any old dress!"

"So you want to run outside half naked?"

"No."

We stuffed our spoiled clothes in the chifforobe. I wore the blue dress and Aaron wrapped the green one around him. We entered the screen porch from the side and peeked through the kitchen door to see if Mom was there. She wasn't. We dashed through the house, into the bathroom and locked the door. I filled the tub with warm water and soap bubbles and let Aaron bathe first, as I stood in the corner, my back to him. I didn't turn from the corner. We didn't speak until I heard him whisper, "your turn." Then he dashed as usual from the bathroom to his bedroom.

After my bath, I cleaned up the bathroom and sprayed it with air freshener. Then I took the dresses back to the storeroom. The place reeked of sour mud. The stench would worsen the longer the soiled clothes were there, but I couldn't think of what to do with them. I opened the little window to let in some fresh air. It helped some, but the window couldn't stay open forever.

On impulse, I bundled up our pants and shirts and shoved them out the window. Then I turned. *Alone with the bone!* I ran my hands over its rough whiteness. My fingers pulsed with the touch. This was something; this amazing discovery was going to change everything. I leaned over it and kissed the top. The dinner bell rang.

Everyone was seated when I came in. I slipped into my chair and waited for Dad to say the blessing. After our plates were filled, Dad asked Mom about Tami. They talked about her determination and how long the experiment might last. Just before dessert was served, Dad looked at Aaron. "What did you do today, son?"

Aaron yawned.

"Come to think of it, I didn't see you or Roberta all day." Mom looked back and forth from Aaron to me.

"You weren't over at that old playhouse, were you? After I told you to stay away?"

"No, Dad. Bertie and I played at . . ."

"We played outside all day, Dad, but we didn't go anywhere near the old playhouse." I interrupted Aaron, afraid he would tell too much. He yawned again.

Mom served apple pie and ice cream and conversation stopped as we ate.

The amazing discovery made me feel special, important. A part of me wanted to tell Dad about it now—to get the nod now. But I waited. If this was done right, I—we—could get more than a nod. Our secret was so stupendous that we might get a smile, words of praise, national fame.

This was big; I could wait.

Chapter 13

The Team

AFTER CHORES THE NEXT MORNING, AARON AND I PLANNED HOW to reveal our amazing discovery. We decided to make a zoo and let the dinosaur bone be the main exhibit. We took dozens of empty mason jars with their metal lids from the storeroom and set them under the oak tree.

We were scientists exploring a newly discovered territory and gathering specimens for identification. The job was dangerous. No one knew which creatures might be poisonous or possess special powers. Only Aaron and I were brave enough to accomplish the task. Scientists from the laboratory team shook our hands and patted our backs as we headed off into the unknown forests, fields, and marshes. No one knew when, or if, we would return.

We found a stink bug on the sheets hanging on the clothesline. In the vegetable garden we unearthed roly-polies and earwigs. In the lush grass between the rock pile and railroad tracks, we found two red racers and a garter snake. In the pasture on the other side of my burned playhouse, we caught grasshoppers and crickets.

Some insects, such as the stink bug and roly-poly, we picked up with our fingers. We grasped the snakes by their tails. We captured yellow jackets and bumblebees by plucking the dandelions or clover on which they lit, dropping the flower, bee and all, into the jar and quickly screwing on the lid.

Trapping red ants was tricky. There was an ant hill as big as a dog house in the forest. But if we disturbed the hill, swarming ants would bite our toes. Instead we caught those that scurried up and down the bark of the oak tree by placing a twig in their path. When they crawled on the twig, we dropped it and the ants into a mason jar and screwed on the lid.

At lunch time, Aaron snuck up by the camper and tossed one of the snakes inside, trying to scare Tami. But Tami didn't scare easily. She shouted through the opened window, "Thanks, Aaron. Just what I needed to control the mice."

We found spiders and a salamander right outside the woodshed. Spiders were captured on a stick the same way we caught the ants. We played with the salamander until it leaped from our hands onto the ground. Aaron was quick enough to catch it again. We looked for the little green frogs that sometimes hid on tree trunks, but couldn't find any.

We had just uncovered a black beetle from under a rotting fence post when the clanking triangle interrupted us. Dinner time already? We raced up the hill to the house. The smell of fried chicken greeted us even before we reached the oak tree. We deposited our jars with the other filled ones at the base of the oak tree and barged onto the screen porch.

"Whoa!" Dad ordered as we slid into our seats at the table. "Go wash up, for crying out loud."

I looked at Aaron. *If Dad thinks we're dirty now, he should have seen us yesterday.* We washed our hands and returned to the dinner table.

"What did you do all day?" Dad asked. It was a routine question.

At dinner time, while we all sat together, Dad discussed issues from the newspaper, told anecdotes about his workday, and always, at some point, asked about our day. He didn't drill us; there was no wrong or right answer. The question was thrown out, and whoever wished, answered it. But it made me nervous.

My fantasy-filled days were too private for discussion. I didn't talk during dinner chats, but I didn't have to. Tami and Aaron always had a lot to say. Tonight Tami was not at the table, and Aaron and I had secrets. What part of our day could we discuss? If Aaron talked, he might reveal too much.

"We collected things," Aaron answered, after swallowing a mouthful of chicken. "We got a bunch of really neat bugs and stuff. We're making a zoo. Tomorrow, we're going to . . ."

"Can we go to the library tomorrow?" I interrupted.

"*May*, not *can*," Dad corrected my grammar without answering my request.

"Hmm," Mom hesitated.

Idiot! I should have given a reason for going before blurting out the request. Mom might refuse, and then it would be forbidden to ask again, reason or not. Another rule in our household was No Arguing with Grown-ups. It was related to No Talking Back and No Cursing.

Tami entered the kitchen. "Thought I'd let you know I gotta go to the library tomorrow for important research." She grabbed a chicken thigh, and left as quickly as she came, the screen door banging behind her.

"Well, I never," Mom began, then stopped. She looked at me and said, "Yes, Roberta. You and Aaron may go to the library with Tamara tomorrow."

Aaron and I grinned at each other.

Bedtime came at the same time whether it was summer vacation or a school night, so I hurried to finish washing the dinner dishes and joined Aaron outside under the oak tree. He was hammering a nail through the lids with a rock, making small air holes for the captured insects and reptiles.

"Better not make one for the ants," I advised. They'd be able to escape through even the tiniest air hole.

"I'm not an idiot," Aaron snapped and continued hammering. I watched him hit the nail with the rock and wondered about his bad mood. He held the nail with one hand and the rock with the other. Clunk! Clunk! The rock hit against the nail. Then "Ouch!" as the rock hit his thumb.

His poor thumb! It was already swollen and the next hit brought a trickle of blood. "Do you want me to try?"

"No. I can do it."

Before going back in the house, we checked on the bone still hidden in the storeroom. Tomorrow was the day. Tomorrow everything would be different. I knew—I absolutely *knew* that the finder of a dinosaur bone would not be a fearful, tongue-tied idiot. Any father would be proud of a child who discovered a dinosaur bone.

Chapter 14

Commies!

DALE WAS NOT MUCH OF A TOWN, BUT IT WAS OUR TOWN. MAIN Street boasted several taverns, an Ace Hardware, a Texaco station, the post office, a barber shop, and a café. Mom and Dad had graduated from Dale High School. Most everyone around was either a relative or a friend of our parents.

We walked the mile to town on the railroad tracks, and crossed at the intersection with the blinking yellow light. The first person we saw was Old Joe. He stood in the middle of the street leaning on his broom talking to an imaginary person. He propped one arm on the broom and gestured with the other as if he were giving directions. Old Joe walked around town with his old broom, sweeping the street, not the sidewalk, and stopping to have conversations with people that only he could see. He was as much a part of our town as the blinking light, taverns, and hardware store. I wondered if Old Joe had pretended things back when he was a kid and just never stopped.

The library shared space with the city hall in a tiny, cinder-block building wedged between the café and the police department. It was dim inside after the bright sunshine. Tami went straight to the card catalogue, while Aaron and I browsed the abbreviated nonfiction section. There were several books on insects and reptiles, but nothing on dinosaurs. I wandered over to the fiction case and ran my hand over every familiar book. Nothing new had been added.

Aaron sat at the single library table engrossed in an insect book. Tami enlisted the help of the librarian to find out something about Jewish customs. The small space felt crowded, so I went back outside.

I watched Old Joe talk and gesture to an invisible friend. Across the street two men left the B & D Tavern, talking loudly and laughing. A passing car honked at them and they turned and waved.

The smell of grilled onions and frying hamburgers escaped from the café next door. A group of men loitered on the sidewalk in front of the café windows.

"They're gonna overtake the country, they will," I heard one man say.

"That's right, and they will do it through our institutions of higher learning," another added.

The conversation was headed down a familiar path guaranteed to spark a fire of fear within me. I should have gone back inside the library or crossed the street. Instead I leaned against the cinder-block wall, and chewed on a strand of hair. Like a moth attracted to light, I strained to hear every word.

"Right now our colleges are full of Communist professors teaching a bunch of nonsense and what does our government do? Not a thing. That's what it does," another man spoke disdainfully.

"By the time our kids are old enough for college, there won't be a good ole U S of A."

If you got kids, mister, how can you let this happen? Do something! The words in my head raced helter-skelter as if they wanted to flee the "Communist professors." How did Communists get in our schools and why didn't someone make them leave?

"We ought to just nuke 'em and git it over with."

No! No! No! Don't nuke them.

"I'll tell you what gets me. We all know they're a bunch of liars, but what does our government do? Wants to sit down and talk with 'em. Now what good is talkin' to a bunch of liars?"

"Tell you what, twenty years from now, the country will be overrun, that's what."

"Naw, we'll all be dead. They'll let go with a bomb, and then we'll let go with one and it'll be one big fireball."

"We oughtta get them afore they get us is all I gotta say."

"Well, I wish Fort Lewis was farther away. Come to war, it'll be a big target and here we are. Can't outrun nuclear fallout. Haven't got enough shelters for everyone. Face it, boys, we're toast."

On the way home, the men's conversation replayed itself in my mind. Fort Lewis was so close that army jeeps traveled through town regularly. I had thought they kept us safe, now I knew they brought danger—and we were in danger enough.

I dawdled behind my brother and sister. Aaron jabbered nonstop about the insect book he'd found, and I wanted to be alone to think.

Why wasn't somebody doing something? I wasn't sure about going to college, but I did want to live. Everywhere there was talk of nuclear war. It was on the news at night, and the adults spoke of it in front of the post office and in the foyer at church.

At home, I avoided Aaron and went straight to my garden. Wilted petals from the dogwood trees littered the moss and ferns. I sat down and toyed with a rusty white flower. I pretended the flower had special protective powers and anyone possessing even a small petal was safe from radiation. I gathered all the fallen, magic petals in a heap and people came from all around to get one from me.

Everyone thought I was wonderful because I had discovered the antidote for nuclear fallout. The men from the café exclaimed over and over how they thought they'd never survive. They thanked me for doing what they could not and argued about whether or not the government should be told. Little children came to hold my hand and sit beside me. Mom found a place with the others under the trees and her eyes were moist with pride. Dad stood beside me and told the crowds, "This is my daughter. Isn't she something!"

Chapter 15

Bad News

AARON DIDN'T ASK WHERE I'D BEEN WHEN I RETURNED FROM MY fantasy escape. He had printed labels in his best penmanship for all our specimens. We got planks from behind the barn and two sawhorses from Dad's shop and made a table between the oak tree and the woodshed. We covered the planks with an old white sheet; Aaron arranged the labeled jars in alphabetical order.

"Let's put the dinosaur bone at the end of the exhibit, like a grand finale," I suggested.

"Yeah," Aaron agreed, "but let's leave it covered and then we can remove the cover like this," he made a grand sweep with his arms, "and the crowd will roar and applaud and lift us up on their shoulders and march around cheering." We both laughed. The big event was scheduled for right after dinner.

Dad was late. He was rarely late, and when he was, it meant bad news. Logging was dangerous and men were sometimes hurt. An injured lumberjack, miles away from medical help, was a serious problem and no one traveled the narrow, winding roads until the wounded man was transported. Being late didn't mean Dad was hurt, but someone was.

I set the table, while Mom put dinner at the back of the stove. I worried—not about an injured logger—but about how much daylight there would be after dinner. Summer days are long in the Northwest, but we wanted to showcase our find in bright daylight, not a dwindling dusk.

Mom returned to the front porch. I went out to ask her how much longer she thought Dad would be, but she sat in the rocker with her hands folded, eyes closed and lips moving. I didn't bother her.

Aaron and I rode our bikes down the lane near the highway. We weren't allowed to cross the railroad tracks, but we could see the road anyway. There was little traffic, and no sign of Dad.

We pedaled our bikes up and down the lane, and we waited.

The ringing of the triangle called us home. We raced back up the hill and put our bikes in the toolshed. The aroma of fresh-baked biscuits beckoned us inside and we bounded up the steps and into the kitchen. Mom gave us each a hot biscuit and we slathered butter on them. I guessed this was to stave off hunger pangs until Dad got home. We never ate dinner without Dad.

"How much longer, Mom?"

"How much longer for what, Roberta?"

"You know. Till Dad gets home."

"Do I look like a fortune teller? How am I supposed to know? He'll get here when he gets here." She clomped out to the front porch.

Why is Mom angry? Did I do something wrong? Tami pushed past me and joined Mom on the porch. Aaron and I grabbed another biscuit and returned to our zoo, but there was nothing to do there.

We climbed the oak tree and sat on a wide branch. Our feet dangled several yards above the ground and the leaves camouflaged our presence. Soon we heard Dad's car rumble to a stop. We peeked through the leaves to see Mom run down the steps. Dad was barely out of the car before Mom hugged him. She clung to him; he rubbed her back and patted it.

Mom and Dad didn't hug often. Happy warmth flooded me from head to toe as I watched them. This was a good day. Soon it would be a great day.

"Ron, I was scared. Really scared this time." Mom stepped back but held Dad's hand and lifted her face toward his.

"I'm not hurt. It wasn't me."

"Not this time. But when you are late from work, someone has been hurt. I pray it isn't you, but I know that if my prayer is answered another wife's prayer is not."

"I'm a logger, Amelia. That's what I am. It's what I do." Dad spoke gruffly, a tired edge to his voice. *Don't be upset, Dad. Don't be unhappy, Mom.* All the fears of the day clutched at my heart and I wanted to run away. I wanted Oma. I peered through the leaves at the covered mound at the end of the make-shift table. Could a dinosaur bone save the day? Dad reached out his hand and brushed a stray wisp of hair out of Mom's face.

She sighed, long and deep. "Well, you've got to be exhausted. Come on inside."

They walked into the house together. Aaron and I climbed down from the branch and wandered over to our insect zoo. I ached to share it with Mom and Dad. Especially now. It would solve everything. Aaron rubbed his hands over the covered bone, then poked his head under the sheet. I giggled. He snarled deep, ferocious dinosaur growls. I laughed harder.

The screen door banged and Tami walked over to us. Aaron came out from under the sheet. Tami picked up a jar with a yellow jacket inside and shook it slightly. The wasp buzzed angrily, trying to sting through the glass.

She picked up every jar, right down the line, read each label and looked carefully at the specimen inside. "This is peachy. Good job, you guys. You could win a science fair with this." Aaron described how we had caught each insect or reptile. He tried to pronounce the scientific names he had painstakingly printed on the labels.

She came to the concealed dinosaur bone. "What's under here?"

Aaron and I looked at each other. Should we show her? Should we wait? We'd waited all day. We'd worked hard at setting up everything and it was already twilight. Maybe if we showed our amazing discovery to Tami, she would run in the house and get Mom and Dad. Maybe the thing Dad was upset about would go away when he saw the dinosaur bone. Maybe Mom would cry out and grab Dad's hand and smile at him.

"Are you ready?" Aaron held a corner of the sheet covering the bone.

"Better stand back." I don't know why I said that. For dramatic effect I guess, but Tami took a step back and Aaron pulled off the sheet with a flourish. Aaron and I shouted together, "Ta-da!"

The bone lay there, large and white and impressive.

"Oh, man! Wow!" Tami ran her hand over the white bone. "Where'd you find this old cow skull?"

Cow skull? *Cow skull!*

"Dug it up in the swamp," Aaron responded. I thought he was going to correct her, that he was going to deny it was a cow skull and defend our dinosaur theory, but he didn't. Neither did I. We didn't look at each other, but stared at the amazing discovery and saw clearly what it was. A cow skull. A stupid, old cow skull.

Chapter 16

Summer Vacation

MOM PUSHED OPEN THE SCREEN DOOR. "COME ON, LET'S EAT."

I should have been hungry, but I wasn't—not even a little. Dad would tell about the hurt logger and I didn't want to hear it.

But I was wrong. Dad didn't talk about his day or even ask about ours. We ate quietly until Aaron broke the silence.

"Guess what, Dad. We have a surprise outside for you after dinner."

"A surprise? What kind of surprise?" Dad kept eating.

"It's a zoo. Well, not a zoo with kangaroos and giraffes, but with bugs and snakes. And something else, too. But that's the biggest surprise." Aaron told about how we collected the insects.

"And wait till you see the grand finale, Dad."

"What is it, son?"

"A really neat surprise. Here's a clue: we found it in the swamp, and me and Bertie worked really hard trying to find . . ."

"Bertie and I worked hard," Dad corrected.

"Yeah. We worked hard and just wait till you see what we found."

How could Aaron still be excited about this? Didn't he realize the whole thing was a bust? There were no dinosaur bones waiting to be discovered, but he jabbered away as if this were the best day ever.

We had worked hard! We had big plans! A scream growled in my head like a cougar deprived of its prey. I chewed on a strand of hair as a tear escaped and I sniffed.

"Do you have something to say, Roberta?" *Why did Mom ask that?* I shook my head no. "May I please be excused?" I hadn't eaten everything on my plate, but I couldn't sit there any longer.

"Ron," Mom spoke softly, patiently. "You know it's been a hard day for all of us. I was a bit cranky while we waited. None of us knew if you were all right or not. Some of us are too sensitive for our own good. You know, Ron?"

Oh, my goodness. Mom thought I was reacting to Dad's tardiness. She saw I was upset and thought I was worried about him. Guilt marched into my heart and sat next to disappointment and failure.

Dad nodded his consent. "You may be excused."

I went to my room. Before long, Mom poked her head in the hallway. "We're going outside, Roberta. Want to come?"

"No."

"Then there's dishes. You get started; Tamara will join you in a few minutes."

While the four of them went outside to inspect the zoo, I cleared the table. *I'm so sick of this. Nothing ever goes right for me. Why can't the bone be a dinosaur? Why does everything have to turn out wrong?* I sniffed and wiped the tears on my sleeve. *You are stupid, Roberta. Too stupid to recognize a cow skull.* The hope of a nod from Dad, the dream of praise vanished like the sun behind a rain cloud.

Summer vacation was not beginning well. But it was summer. Summer! Time for picnics and swimming in the lake at Grandma Benson's. Summer meant Kool-aid popsicles, carrots straight from the garden, playing in the sprinkler, and floating on inner tubes down the Deschutes River near Cougar Mountain.

The day after the dinosaur fiasco, Aaron and I went to the daisy-filled meadow behind the house while Tami worked on her "award-winning" play. A group of young fir trees formed an irregular circle near the edge of the field. Aaron and I dragged old fence posts to the middle of the circle and built a fort. It was square with one post on top of the other, like Lincoln Logs, but our posts were not notched so there were large gaps between each log. To get inside, we climbed up the posts and jumped through the roof—if there had been a roof. We poked stick rifles through the gaps in the walls and defended the fort from renegades.

When we came back to the house for lunch, Tami was frowning on the back porch steps. "What's the matter?" I was surprised to see her out of the trailer.

"We're going *camping* this weekend." She pronounced *camping* as if it were a dirty word.

"Yea!" Aaron shouted and jumped.

When Dad got home from work on Friday, he towed the camp trailer to Lake Cushman. The next morning, we hiked up Staircase, through an old growth forest. Rotting logs criss-crossed the hillside where tiny rivulets flowed through bracken, sword, and deer ferns. Multicolored fungus grew on decaying stumps; mushrooms hid under towering trees. *If gnomes or fairies or leprechauns existed, they would live here.* What if they did? What if I discovered a colony of little people? Would that be as impressive as finding a dinosaur bone? More impressive?

I loved this enchanted forest. Tiny, white, star-shaped flowers grew along the needle-cushioned path. The deep stillness made me want to step softly and whisper. It was like my secret garden only more majestic, more magical.

"It's so beautiful." Tami must have felt the same way because she spoke in a whisper.

"Beautiful? You think dead and decaying is beautiful?" Dad's verbal attack intruded on the solemnity of the trail. "I'll tell you what's beautiful. A new forest that sustains life, where the deer nibble on tender tree tops and things are growing, not dying." Dad kicked a rotten cedar log. His words startled me. *He doesn't think this forest is beautiful and enchanting?*

"Do you see any young fir trees here? No you don't. Do you know why? Because fir won't grow in the shade. So this beautiful forest, as you call it, won't stay evergreen. It'll be taken over by alder and maple, junk wood."

Tami debated boldly. "Yes, Dad, the old-growth forest will die and be replaced by deciduous trees which also provide food for deer and squirrels and all kinds of birds."

"Houses aren't built out of alder. Douglas fir is the money crop and there isn't anything prettier than a growing, well-managed Douglas fir forest."

I ran ahead of Dad and Tami. I didn't want to listen to an argument about old-growth versus new-growth. The magic spell had been shattered, and I wanted it back. It shocked me that something this beautiful was somehow bad. Or was it?

I charged ahead of the arguing until I reached a footbridge spanning a boulder-strewn river. Surging water crashed against rocks and fallen trees, as if nothing could stop its race downstream. The noise thundered louder than the seashore; spray dampened my hair; the air smelled fresh. I leaned over the bridge's wooden rail. The wild water captivated me as much as the solemn forest, but in a different way; the turbulent current felt the opposite of the serene forest, yet here they lived, side by side. Chaos and peace.

Around the campfire that night, Dad stood and cleared his throat. "I've got an announcement."

I stopped roasting a marshmallow and looked at him. *Is this a good announcement?*

Mom sat up straighter and smiled as if she was already in on the secret.

"Monday morning I start a new position with Weyerhaeuser. I won't be in the woods anymore; I'm an office man now."

"Wow, Dad. That's a big change." Tami's smile was as big as Mom's.

"I'll be getting home late for about six weeks. There's an accounting class I have to take in Tacoma."

Aaron clapped. I didn't know why he was clapping, but I joined him, then Mom and Tami clapped too. "Thanks." Dad left our circle and began pumping up the Coleman lantern, his back to us.

Monday morning he wore a dark blue suit and smelled like Old Spice instead of fir trees. Mom said he was handsome. He wore jeans and a hickory shirt on the weekend.

His late hours meant no CBS news in the evening. It also meant I couldn't ride my bike for a while. For most of three days, Aaron and I had played cops and robbers on our bicycles, racing around the gravel lanes that led out to the highway, around the large circle between our house and my old playhouse and back and forth between the barn, garage, and Dad's shop. Aaron and I were the cops and the bad guys were imaginary, but we'd head them off at an intersection or chase them out of the county as we sped down the hill toward the highway. But a nail punctured my tire and I needed Dad to patch it. Mom said it would have to wait for the weekend.

Aaron and I made the playhouse into a clubhouse. We tried to get Tami to join our secret society, but she brushed us aside with an excuse about her writing. We barricaded the storeroom door and I read aloud from Aaron's favorite book, *Treasure Island*, while he acted out the scenes. The drama sometimes left me breathless. We pretended we were part of the Pickwick Club like the characters in *Little Women* and "reported" on our amazing adventures and exotic travels during secret club meetings.

On the Fourth of July we watched the parade as usual, then had a picnic in Pioneer Park. After we ate, we walked through the midway where tinny music blared from scratchy speakers, and the sweet smell of cotton candy mingled with the greasy odor of fried elephant ears. I pretended not to see Carol, a classmate from last year, helping her mother at the hot-dog stand. What if I waved to her and she ignored me?

When the sky darkened, everyone spread blankets on the ground transforming the park into a huge patchwork quilt. I squeezed between Tami and Aaron and we lay on our backs eager for the fireworks display. We "ooohed" and "aaahed" with each bright burst exploding directly overhead. It seemed as if the falling lights could land right on us, but none of them did. The fireworks made me think about nuclear fallout. Maybe somebody could make a rule that the radiation had to be colored so we could tell if we were in danger. It wouldn't have to be pretty colors, just something so we could see the "bombs bursting in air," so we could see where it fell.

As the warm July days passed, I grew restless and irritable. Window-rattling detonations from Fort Lewis jolted my nerves. Army jeeps daily chugged along the highway, reminding me over and over of the danger we were in. I flinched with every artillery blast; I caught my breath with the sight of each military convoy.

But that wasn't all that bothered me. I didn't like the green color of my bicycle. I hated my braids. I did not, could not, play dolls anymore, and no matter how Aaron begged, I had no interest in building forts or playing with his Tonka toys.

From the kitchen window, I watched Aaron play football by himself. As the quarterback he threw the ball down the field, then as the receiver he caught it and raced away for a touchdown. Sometimes he was tackled, sometimes he made it to the end zone. It wasn't hard to tell which had happened: when tackled he fell down hard, rose slowly, and stood up dejected; if he made it into the end zone, he spiked the ball, raised both hands in victory and bowed to the crowd. I watched him and knew there was room for me in the game, but I didn't want to play, *couldn't* play, and I didn't know why.

I could think of a hundred things I didn't want to do, but not a single thing that I did want to do.

Chapter 17

No Bomb Shelter

UNLESS WE WERE CAMPING, FRIDAY WAS GAME NIGHT AT THE SWANsens. While Mom and Mrs. Swansen challenged Dad and Mr. Swansen to pinochle, Tami and Willie played Monoply on the porch, and Aaron and Carl played in the orchard or in the hayloft. I usually joined the younger boys, but lately, I hadn't felt like it.

"Come on, Bertie. We need a third person." Aaron waited by the open barn door.

I pretended not to hear him, and went around to the font porch. Tami and Willie sat on a wicker settee, with a Monopoly game on a low table in front of them. Willie had his arm across the back of the settee as if he wanted to put it around Tami. I leaned against a square pillar at the top of the stairs and cleared my throat.

"What do you want?" Willie looked embarrassed, as if I'd caught him doing something he shouldn't. He put his arm down.

"May I play?" I'd never asked to play before because Monopoly was boring, but maybe now—now that playing in the hayloft was boring—maybe I would like it. Shouldn't a game with colored money and miniature shoes be fun?

It wasn't. They let me play, but before my wheelbarrow had

rounded the board five times, I'd been in jail twice and paid luxury tax, but owned no two properties of the same color. All my green and yellow and pink and blue money sat in front of Tami and Willie.

Next Friday night, I'll bring a book. I went in the house.

"Roberta, help yourself to pie." Mrs. Swansen gestured to me from the kitchen. The house smelled like apples and cinnamon and fresh-baked bread.

Mr. Swansen spoke in a deep voice. "You can cut a piece for me too."

"You've already had one," Mrs. Swansen scolded.

"Yep, I did. And I'm going to have another." His laugh boomed through the kitchen. "Just like Ron and I won one game, and we're going to win another."

"Oh, you." Mrs. Swansen's dark blue eyes flashed behind her glasses.

I served the pie to the adults. Apple pie was Dad's favorite and if Mr. Swansen could have two pieces, so could Dad.

Eating in the living room was not allowed, and I didn't want to go back to the porch with Tami and Willie, so I sat on a kitchen stool and ate my pie at the counter. The adults played their game and talked.

"Have you started that bomb shelter yet, Ron?" Mr. Swansen had a shelter in his basement. Last month he had taken us down to it and showed off the provisions.

Dad didn't answer him. He flipped a red ace in the center of the table, then raked all the cards towards himself.

Mrs. Swansen looked at Mom. "You know, you really need one. Radiation poisoning is nothing to fool around with. Why, you can get poisoned and not even know it's in the air." She shook her head. "It's an awful way to die."

Mom discarded a red ten. "I heard that as long as you find shelter quickly, you should be all right." She glanced at me and smiled.

Mr. Swansen slapped a black jack on the table. "That's what we're saying. You need a shelter you can get to quickly." Mr. Swansen couldn't help talking loud. It was the only volume he had.

I felt like I did when I had eavesdropped outside the library. My palms were sweaty, my heart thrummed in my ears, and the pie stuck in my throat. But I sat silently, latching on to every word.

Mrs. Swansen put her hand on Mom's arm. "Amelia, I'm telling you, exposure to radiation is horrendous. You can get painful beta burns, headaches to drive one crazy, stomach wrenching heaves, excruciating pain. Then you die."

I dropped my fork.

Mom's voice shook slightly. "Well, we can keep our doors and windows shut tight."

"Maybe if you had heavy drapes, but those lacey things you have hardly keep out the sun, let alone gamma rays." Usually I liked to hear Mr. Swansen talk, but I wanted him to stop now. He didn't. His voice reverberated not just through the room, but into my bones.

I wanted to scream at them. *Then do something! Don't just talk about radiation, stop it from happening.*

Dad finally spoke up. "We know what you're saying. We've heard the same reports." He ticked off each point on his fingers. "An underground, concrete basement is best, but an earthen one will work; emergency kits should contain fresh batteries and plenty of water; flashlights are better than candles, but have both; light colors repel radiation, while dark absorbs it; a radio is essential." He sounded like he was reciting a boring homework assignment.

He shuffled the cards, then dealt them. "We've heard it all again and again. What we don't know is if any of it matters. We don't really know that anything we do will make any difference."

No one answered.

It won't matter? Preparations won't matter? Why not? They have to matter!

If Dad refused to prepare for nuclear war, then what hope was there? Maybe nothing anyone did could help, but wasn't it worth a try? *What can I do?*

Prepare the storeroom. Why hadn't I thought of it before? It already held jars of food. It had a concrete floor and no daylight showed around the door when it was closed. I could put the yellow and white quilt over the window.

When the bombs came, I'd have to get the portable toilet from the camper and the emergency medical kit from the bathroom. I could grab the radio from the kitchen, but fresh batteries might be a problem. I wished I could gather everything ahead of time. Minutes spent after a bomb dropped would risk exposure to radiation. How could I be safe and still get everything we needed?

Light-colored clothes were the answer. Dad said light colors repelled radiation. I'd have to always wear white, or at least pastels. I looked at the red blouse and blue jeans I had on. Where was I going to get light-colored clothes?

Chapter 18

The Nest

I HAD JUST NAILED THE QUILT OVER THE WINDOW IN THE STORE-room when clanging from the triangle called me to the house. Fill-ing the three empty jugs with water would have to wait.

"Tamara, I need to take your measurements. Roberta, you too." Mom held a measuring tape in one hand and a pattern in the other. Disappointment from being called away from the storeroom melted with the prospect of new, light-colored school clothes. Mom was the best seamstress in the world. When she sewed, I often perched on a stool nearby watching her fingers manipulate the fabric, impatient for the finished dress.

As she opened the sewing cabinet that sultry, late afternoon in August, I was eager for what was to come. I did not expect poison-laced oatmeal to spill out of every nook and cranny in the cabinet and machine itself.

The poison Dad and I put out! "Oh my goodness!" I clapped my hands to my mouth. Instead of eating the oatmeal, the crazy mice had stored it away for a winter feast.

Mom slumped on her sewing chair. "Oh, no. My beautiful

machine. Oh, no." She opened the narrow top drawer. More poison. The middle drawer. Poison again. The bottom drawer.

"Aaaaaaaah!" Mom screamed.

"Aaaaaaaaaaaaaah!" I screamed.

A large mouse jumped out, right at Mom. It landed on her foot, then scurried past her, but its way was blocked by a pantry cupboard. It pivoted and dashed between my legs. "Aaaaaaaaah!"

Mom grabbed a broom and whacked at it. She missed, but the mouse changed direction again and ran along the baseboard. Tami bumped into me, trying to get out of its way.

I jumped up on Mom's stool. "Aaaaaaaaah!"

"Roberta, stop screaming. Tamara, help me." Mom whisked the broom along the floor. The mouse leaped onto the broom and off again. Aaron joined the chaos, trying to stomp on the mouse with his boots.

I covered my mouth with both hands to hold in the screams. Memories of Mr. Darcy flooded my mind. I desperately wanted this mouse to live, but I couldn't move. I couldn't save it.

Tami grabbed a flannel shirt from the mending basket and threw it on top of the mouse. The flannel wiggled slightly, but the hectic scurrying stopped. Aaron raised his foot to stomp on it; Tami pushed him away.

"No!" she shouted. She scooped the mouse, shirt and all into a clean gallon milk jar from the counter and quickly screwed on the wide lid. "Poor little thing," she crooned.

"Poor little thing, my foot!" panted Mom. "Did you see what that 'poor little thing' did to my sewing machine? It's a nasty, horrible thing." She spat out the words, her eyes blazing and cheeks flushed. "Aaron, kill it. Just take it out of here and kill it."

Tami raised the jar above her head—out of Aaron's reach—and ran out of the kitchen, through the screen porch, down the steps, and into the yard. Near the apple tree she unscrewed the metal lid and dumped out the contents. She grabbed a corner of the shirt and the mouse tumbled away. In a jiffy it was lost in the thick, overgrown grass.

Aaron and I had followed Tami outside, but Mom remained behind. We trooped back into the kitchen, Tami carrying the empty jar, Aaron scuffling his feet, and I wary of what was to come. Mom might collapse into a chair and erupt into contagious laughter, but what would she find funny about a ruined sewing machine and Tami's disobedience? We found Mom in the pantry, looking at something in the drawer from which the mouse had escaped.

She removed the narrow drawer and carried it with both hands through the kitchen. "Aaron, come with me. Tamara, you stay here."

From the kitchen window, Tami and I saw her dump the contents on the gravel driveway. Mystified, we watched as Aaron rode back and forth over the area on his bicycle. And then we realized what we were seeing. Mixed in with the gravel were the remains of a mouse nest: shredded bits of newspaper; fragments of cloth; and tiny, naked, squirming baby mice.

Tami shrieked and dashed to her room. I didn't know how to feel. I hated the panicked mouse loose in our house. I hated what had happened to Mom's sewing machine. I was relieved when Tami defiantly freed it, but I understood that she shouldn't have. The mouse would easily find its way back into the house and the damage it had caused, the damage it could cause again, was serious.

The sight of the helpless, writhing babies being crushed under the wheels of my brother's bicycle was sickening. Nauseated, I shut myself in the bathroom and sobbed.

I heard Tami's door creak open and Mom's voice. "Young lady, you will stay right here until your father gets home."

When Mom left, I stood in front of Tami's closed door. I wanted to tell her I was glad she had freed the mouse, that what Aaron and Mom had done was terrible, but I couldn't open her door. I hadn't gone in since Oma died—and I still couldn't go in, not even to comfort my sister. I couldn't even touch the doorknob.

The rattle of pots and pans signaled Mom was preparing dinner. I didn't want to be in the same room with her. *Where can I go?* Aaron was probably playing outside, but I didn't want to see him either. I went back in the bathroom and locked the door. I sat on the edge of the tub and when an artillery blast from Fort Lewis shook the window, I cried. I cried for the dead mice and for Oma, for my burnt playhouse and for the games I didn't want to play anymore. I cried because Fort Lewis was too near and nuclear war was too possible. I cried because I didn't want to wear braids.

I didn't hear Dad's car drive up the lane. I didn't hear his voice or Mom's as she related the day's events, but I knew he was home and I knew Mom had told him because I heard his footsteps in the hallway.

"Tamara. Let's go." The woodshed. Again.

I washed my face, undid my braids, and brushed my hair. I tiptoed through the living room, out the front door, and headed for the dogwood trees. *It's okay. It's gonna be okay.* I stopped halfway to my garden, detouring to the swing in the old maple tree. Back and forth I swung, gently, lazily. *Poor mice babies.* Then I saw the squirming shapes again in my mind. *Go away, stupid mice!* I pumped the swing hard. The motion brought me closer to the blue, blue heavens. I leaned way back in the swing until my long hair brushed the ground and I could see the highest branches of the tree making patterns against the azure sky.

I peered through the branches and wondered if God knew about

our troubles. Did He care? I wanted to talk to Him, really talk to
Him, but I didn't know how. I knew the prayers we recited before
our meals and the ones we repeated in church but right now, just
at this time, they didn't feel right. I tried anyway and spoke aloud,
"Our Father which art in heaven." The swing slowed. "Hallowed be
Thy name." I felt nothing. I might as well be talking to the trees or
the sky.

"Please, God," I cried aloud. *Please what? What do I want to ask
God? What do I want?* I swung back and forth and let the rhythm of
the swing soothe me. The words in my head settled down. *What do
I want? If God were listening, what would I tell Him?*

I imagined God sitting in the maple tree, looking at me. I couldn't
see His face, but I knew He was there and that He was paying attention to me. Even so, the words wouldn't come out right. Feelings
scrambled my brain. God waited, obscured by the branches of the
tree, until I was ready.

"This is the way it is," I spoke aloud as if I were talking to Oma
in bed. "I want to please my dad and I can't. I want him to be proud
of me, to notice me, and everything turns out wrong. I am afraid of
him and I don't want to be. I cry all the time and I hate it. No one is
doing anything about the Cubans and the Commies and I'm scared.
I don't want them to take over the world and I don't want to die by a
nuclear bomb. Mom is grouchy and I don't know why and now I'm
scared of her." The words hung in the air, then floated up through
the branches of the tree.

An enormous hand reached down through the leaves and lifted
me from the swing into the cloudless sky. I rose, higher and higher,
cradled in the massive palm.

The hand deposited me in the pocket of a red and black plaid coat.
It smelled of fir needles just like Dad's mackinaw. I peered from the

pocket and the world whizzed past. We were everywhere at once. And everywhere we turned our presence made a difference. Chaos became harmony. A swirl of color became a rainbow. Yelling and fighting and screaming turned into melodious music. War machines and nuclear bombs transformed into paintings of a beautiful countryside. Crumbled buildings became crystal palaces floating on silvery clouds.

I laughed and a deep voice laughed with me.

Clanging from the dinner triangle broke the spell. The swing slowed and I jumped from it and skipped back home. Was that a rainbow lingering in the sky? Were the birds singing just for me? I bounded up the steps and into the house, but dinner was a quiet affair. No one answered Dad's question about how our day went, not even Aaron. Before the meal was over, the heaviness of the afternoon returned in force.

I went to bed feeling restless. The ticking of the cuckoo clock paced the minutes as the hours slogged by. Then my pulse quickened as through my open bedroom door, I spied a mouse creeping furtively along the baseboard in the hallway. He darted behind the door and then emerged again slowly, steadily advancing toward me.

"Dad!" I shouted. "There's a mouse! Aaron! A mouse, a mouse!"

No one answered my call.

Was it the mouse Tami had freed? It saw me watching. I wanted to wave my arms to frighten it away, but they wouldn't move. The mouse inched closer and scuttled up the bed frame. I kicked my feet and thrashed about trying to scare it away, but it kept coming. I pressed my back against the headboard and brought my knees under my chin; the mouse did not retreat. He edged closer and closer until he was right at my feet. Sharp teeth nibbled on my toes. I raised my nightie to kick him away, but lace doilies flopped where my feet should have been.

My own screams woke me.

I bolted upright in bed. "Mom!" Her room was too far for her to hear me. Aaron's form was obscure in the murky darkness, but I could hear his rhythmic breathing.

"Aaron!" His breathing remained unchanged. "Aaron!" Still no response.

I was afraid to go back to sleep. What if a real mouse came?

Rain pellets hit against the window. I liked rain; it was somehow comforting. I snuggled down in my bed, but pictured myself going outside.

I raised my face to the friendly, familiar rain and settled on the swing. I pumped higher and higher and, joy! The great hand swooped down and put me in the mackinaw's pocket where we flew through rainbows and swirls of color and silvery mists. Once again chaos and destruction transformed into harmony and beauty. When I awoke the terror of the first dream had been diluted to a vague, hazy memory.

The smell of frying bacon awakened hunger pangs. I got up and stepped over Aaron on the floor. Mom's light giggles in unison with Dad's deep, short laugh came from behind the kitchen door. I didn't want to interrupt them so I waited and listened.

There's no better sound than my parents laughing together.

Chapter 19

Going for the Light

SATURDAY DAD CLEANED THE POISON-PACKED SEWING MACHINE and got it running again. Mom spent the next two weeks catching up with her sewing, but she couldn't make new shoes. Aaron hated shopping so much that he tried to pretend his toes weren't cramped in last year's boots. The truth was we'd run barefoot all summer and there was no way any of us could squeeze into last year's footwear.

I wasn't excited about new shoes either. Mom believed in prudent, not stylish, purchases. While other girls showed off their Mary Janes or penny loafers, I wore saddle shoes. They were sturdy, but not at all pretty and I'd rather go barefoot.

I was excited about getting a new coat.

My old school jacket was a sensible, chestnut brown. I planned to have a new coat in as light a color as Mom would allow—white if possible—but there was no way I could settle for a dark-colored coat. Not even if dark fabrics were in style. Not even if they were the cheapest price. I didn't want a dark-colored coat because I wanted to live.

I wanted a long, light-colored coat with a hood. If the Commies attacked while I was at school, I could run the mile home. Maybe I could survive if I had a jacket with pockets for my hands and a hood to cover my head and a light enough color to repel the fallout. If it happened while I was at home, I needed the coat for protection while I gathered provisions from the house and camper and took them to the storeroom. I'd surely die in a dark, radiation-absorbing coat.

The windshield wipers had a hard time keeping up with the rain the afternoon Mom drove us to Olympia for our shoes and coats. Tami sat in the front with her. Aaron and I sat in the back. Aaron kicked the back of Mom's seat.

"Aaron, sit still."

Please, Aaron, I silently pleaded. *Please don't upset Mom.* I needed her to be in a good, understanding mood. My plan had little chance of success if she was grouchy.

Our yearly shopping trip to Olympia could have been a treat, but money was tight. We didn't browse through the stores choosing what was prettiest or what we liked best. We bought what we needed, what was the most sensible, the most durable, the best value for the dollar. I liked pretty things. Mom did too. But when it came to footwear, durable beat pretty every time.

"Why do they insist on one-way streets in this town?" Mom circled the block again. "Tami, help me look for a parking spot. A big one. Maybe on a corner." There was an edge to Mom's voice. Every year it was the same thing; we all knew how much she disliked the downtown traffic; we'd experienced her failed attempts at parallel parking.

She went around the block again and finally found a big spot on the corner. Aaron fed pennies to the parking meter, then we dashed through the rain and pushed open the double glass doors with "J. C. Penney" printed in gold block letters. Aaron hurried to a candy counter under the escalator. Dainty chocolates and taffy lined the shelves. I breathed in the smells of fudge and caramel.

"Hey, Mom!" Aaron pressed his nose against the glass display case. I knew he was thinking a bag of candy would ease the pain of shopping.

"No, Aaron. Come on. Stay with me." Mom spoke sharply. Was she still unnerved by the traffic and crowded streets?

Aaron straggled behind, looking back every step or two at the candy. Mom grabbed his hand and jerked him along. He was too old to have to hold her hand in a store, but he didn't pull away.

I thought we'd go to footwear first, but Mom led us to the fabric department, a section of the store Aaron especially detested.

"I'm here to pick up fabric set aside for Amelia Thorne." The clerk gave her a huge bundle of heavy, off-white material.

"Oh, Mom, I love this," Tami exclaimed. "It will make beautiful drapes for the living room."

I dropped the braid from my mouth and smiled. *New drapes out of almost-white fabric? Thank you, Mr. Swansen!*

Footwear was on the first floor. As I expected, Mom picked out two-toned brown saddle shoes for me, and black-and-white ones for Tami. Tami protested. "I hate these, Mom. Nobody in high school wears these."

Mom ignored her.

Tami pouted as the salesman used a horn to force on the stiff shoes. "Someday when I'm a famous playwright, I'll have enough money to buy whatever shoes I want."

"Stand up." Mom knelt to feel the end of her toes. We always bought footwear with room to grow because one pair lasted the entire school year. The shoes started out too big, and ended up too snug, but for most of the year they fit fine. Even I could see how two pair of shoes in one year was an extravagance.

I looked longingly at black, patent leather Mary Janes with a bow on the strap, but I saved my protest for the coat. I wished Tami and Aaron would cooperate. If they put Mom in a bad mood before we finished with the shoes, it would be even harder to convince her to buy me a light-colored coat. Dark brown did not show playground dirt.

Aaron didn't care what kind of boots he had, but he wiggled and squirmed and made it difficult for the salesman to fit him. Mom was grumpy. "Aaron, stop it, now!"

With the shoes in shopping bags, we headed for the escalator. Aaron stalled at the candy counter, but Mom firmly nudged him to move on. She didn't promise him a treat if he behaved because that wasn't the way things were done. We were expected to "be good." If we disobeyed, were disrespectful, or broke the rules, we were disciplined. We were not rewarded for doing what we ought.

Mom didn't give Aaron any hope of candy, but that didn't stop him from wanting some. I understood how much he hated shopping, so I should have known he'd cause trouble. I should have done something to prevent the disaster that followed.

Upstairs, the coats hung on circular frames. Aaron scooted through the jackets on a sale rack and hid in the middle of the display. The coats concealed him, but I could see his eyes peering out through a slit at the top of the rack. Mom approached the display and at the exact moment that she reached for the sales tag dangling from a jacket sleeve, Aaron poked between the coats, grabbed her arm, and growled.

Mom screamed.

Aaron ducked back under the coats and dropped to his knees. He might have crawled away, but Mom was too quick for him. She grabbed his ankle and yanked him toward her, but his leg caught the base of the display. When she jerked him, the rack toppled toward her. It knocked Mom off balance and she landed flat on her bottom. She sat with her legs stretched out, coats piled on top of her. A fuzzy red jacket draped over her face. Aaron's legs flailed about under a pile of yellow rain slickers.

When Tami burst out laughing, I couldn't help but join her. Mom tried to pull off the red jacket, but her head was caught in a sleeve and her struggles made it worse. We stifled our giggles as I helped Aaron up and Tami assisted Mom. My smile disappeared when I saw the look on Mom's face.

We were never disciplined in public, but we never escaped paying for our misdeeds. Mom did not yell at Aaron or spank him. She whispered in his ear and clutched his arm while two laughing sales clerks righted the stand and returned the crumpled coats to the rack. Mom stood Aaron against the bare wall by the escalator where she could see him and ordered him to stay put. He appeared contrite, but I knew his face could be deceiving. I also knew the damage had already been done. My chances of convincing Mom of anything were nil. Zip. Zilch. Nada.

Still, I had to try.

"Mom," I began tentatively. Only a hoarse peep squeaked past my tight throat. I swallowed and began again. "Mom."

I waited for her to acknowledge me. Her attention was divided between Aaron and Tami who was looking at fake fur coats hanging against the wall. They were all very dark; some were actually black and none of them looked the least bit sensible, certainly not machine washable. Maybe when Mom was done with Tami, she would be in a better mood.

I rummaged through a sale rack, passing over one dark coat after another. And then, on the third stand I found it: calf-length, zip-out fleece lining, water-resistant, a removable hood, machine washable, and the softest, palest sherbet-lime green. It was so perfect that I was a little surprised not to see a tag dangling from the sleeve declaring the fabric "radiation repellent." I tried it on.

I made my way over to where Tami was trying on a sporty, dark blue pea coat. I waited as Mom checked the arm length, the quality of the fabric and stitching. Tami turned this way and that, scrutinizing her reflection in a narrow mirror attached to a post. The coat brought out the deep blue of her eyes and made her wavy hair appear more blonde. It fit her well. Mom looked pleased.

She turned my way, but her eyes went past me. I turned to follow her gaze at the empty wall by the escalator. Aaron was gone.

Mom pursed her lips and furrowed her brow, staring at the vacant spot where Aaron should have been.

I looked under display racks and Tami headed for the dressing rooms. "Aaron! Aaron!" I called.

Mom walked over and touched my arm. "Don't." That's all she said.

Tami returned from the dressing room, shaking her head.

Mom took her wallet out of her purse and gave it to Tami. "Go pay for your coats," she said and whisked to the escalators.

Of course. He's at the candy counter. As Tami and I waited in the checkout line, it hit me. Instead of Aaron making it impossible for me to negotiate with Mom, he had made it unnecessary! I hugged the coat close. I was going to live! Tami paid the sales clerk, thanked her, and then, packages in hand, we hurried to the escalator.

Mom was talking to the candy clerk as we walked up. I didn't see Aaron anywhere.

"He isn't here?" Tami looked as surprised as I felt.

"No. He isn't here."

"Well," Tami began.

Mom interrupted. "I want to get home before dark. Come on, girls."

I was dumbstruck. *We are going to leave Aaron here? We can't do that! This is Olympia! We can't just go off and leave him. It isn't safe! It isn't right!* As we headed for the double glass doors, I looked around frantically, trying to get a glimpse of him somewhere. I bumped into an elderly gentleman entering the store, but I couldn't even think to say, "Excuse me."

I stopped in front of the doors. *I'm not leaving. I'm staying here with my brother.* Mom would have to drag me kicking and screaming to the car, but I was not going to abandon Aaron. *Where is he? How can I stay with him if I can't find him?* There were no coat racks to conceal him. There were shoes and purses and men's shirts on flat tables, but I saw nowhere that my brother could hide.

Did he go out to the car? If he is at the car and I'm not will Mom leave me? I pushed through the double glass doors and caught up with Mom and Tami. They were talking, but the sounds from the street drowned their conversation.

Aaron was not at the car. I looked back up the street, hoping he would come running after us, but there was no sign of him. *Aaron where are you?* I knew he wouldn't stand alone by the wall, so why hadn't I kept an eye on him, or ask him to help me find a coat or think of some game to keep him occupied? I should have done something.

Standing on the sidewalk in the drizzling rain, I wanted to refuse to leave without him, to demand we go back and find him. This was crazy! The words of protest formed in my head, jumbled together, and mixed themselves up like pebbles rolled by waves on the beach. I stammered and stuttered, but uttered nothing intelligible.

"Get in the car, Roberta." Mom unlocked the door. I dawdled, fumbling with my packages, stalling for time. Another look up the street. No Aaron.

Tami chatted with Mom in the front seat. I knew she didn't care when Aaron got into mischief and was sent to the woodshed, but how could she not care now? *This is serious! What is Mom thinking?*

Mom started the car. *No! Mom, please don't do this!* My mouth formed the words, but no sound came out. Soon the signal lights and city traffic were behind us. We whizzed along the darkening highway, farther and farther from my brother. *Where is he now? Is he safe? What will he do if he leaves his hiding place and can't find us? Will he leave the store? Will he roam the streets of Olympia, lost and alone? Will he freeze to death huddled in a dark doorway?*

He leaves his hiding place and searches the first floor, but can't find us. He rides the escalator upstairs, still looking for us. Not believing that we'd leave him, he braves the women's restroom sure that we are hiding from him there. The attendant cleaning the stalls accosts him and calls security. "Boys aren't allowed in a women's restroom," she scolds him. A burly man grabs him by the back of his neck and takes him to the store manager.

He tries to explain that he has been left behind by his mother, but no one believes him. "Mothers don't leave their children behind." The manager tapes his mouth with duct tape to keep him quiet. The police handcuff him, and haul him off to jail. He is allowed one phone call, but we aren't home. They take his fingerprints and make a file with his name on it and the words "Juvenile Delinquent."

I startled from my daydream when Mom turned off the car engine. Dad's car was parked by the shop; what would he say when Mom told him she'd left Aaron behind?

I fumbled with the door handle and dropped my packages several times before I could get out of the car and close the door. I jumped out of Dad's way as he took the porch stairs two at a time, jumped in the station wagon and revved the motor. Tires spun in the gravel as he raced off back the way we had come.

Anger rose within me. *Why did Aaron pull such a stunt? Why did Mom abandon him? Why didn't Tami care?* I was even angry with Dad, but I didn't know why. I stomped up the porch steps and let the screen door bang shut behind me.

Tami already had her new coat out of the bag and was modeling it in the kitchen. I dropped my packages on the floor. I wanted the drop to make an impression, to make a loud thud, but the coat cushioned the fall of the shoebox, and they landed with an unremarkable, soft rustle.

Still, I got Mom's attention. I didn't even try to hide my anger. I didn't care if I was being insolent. "How could you!" I meant to shout, but the words squeaked out, broken and high-pitched.

Mom sat down on a kitchen chair. "Come here."

As I approached her, she looked steadily in my eyes. I tried to stare back, strong and defiant, but tears weakened my resolve, and I couldn't look at her. I didn't want to cry, I wanted to accuse!

"Roberta. Roberta, look at me." I lifted my head, but I didn't meet her eyes. I focused on her mouth.

"Roberta, you are a foolish girl. I do not have to defend my actions to you, but I will explain what is happening. Aaron is a strong-willed, mischievous boy. He must learn a lesson. I hope he thinks he was left behind on his own, but the truth is Mildred is watching him. You remember the clerk at the candy counter? She is an old school friend of mine and she won't let him get hurt."

Mom took both my hands in hers and gently squeezed them. "He has a lesson to learn, and this should do it. Mildred won't let him leave the store until your father arrives, and if Aaron gets scared, well, that's all the better." She put her hands on my shoulders and patted them lightly.

"Things are not always what they seem. Remember that, Roberta."

Mom and Tami rustled pots and pans in the kitchen. I sat in the dark on Aaron's bed. Mom was confident that Aaron was safe; I was not. I perked up when car tires crunched on the gravel and two doors shut. There was a delay before I heard footsteps in the hallway—a delay undoubtedly caused by a detour to the woodshed.

During dinner Tami jabbered about the shopping trip. As she rambled on, I saw Dad and Aaron look at each other from across the table. Dad nodded at him and Aaron nodded back. I saw the understanding look pass between them. Whatever happened in the woodshed tonight must not have been too bad.

And the best part of the day's end was my beautiful, light-colored coat hung in the closet.

Chapter 20

School!

AFTER OUR LABOR DAY CAMPING TRIP, DAD PARKED THE CAMPER
under a shelter near his shop. A sky blue ribbon held Tami's hand-
written play together. She put the bundle in a shirt box and slid it
under her bed.

"When do we get to read it?" Mom asked at dinner.

"Not yet. Later. I read somewhere that I should put it away and read
it again a month or more later. It said I would view it with 'fresh eyes.'"

"So in a month?" Mom was insistent.

"If it's good enough." Tami's voice sounded self-confident even
if her words showed doubt. She slept in her room that night for the
first time all summer. I didn't join her. At first I had thought I just
didn't want to be alone in the room, but even with Tami there, I
couldn't go in.

Tuesday was the first day of school! We had purchased our school
supplies at Warden's, and in last year's pencil box I had two freshly
sharpened pencils and a new, pink pearl eraser. I put a third of a
sheaf of wide-ruled paper in my old green binder and placed everything in my book bag.

Tuesday morning I wore a light blue, print dress Mom made, but it was too warm for my new coat, so I contented myself with Tami's hand-me-down, cream-colored cardigan. Aaron ran down the lane toward the bus stop, but my new shoes were too stiff for running and I couldn't keep up with him.

"Hurry up, you guys! I see the bus!" Aaron yelled back at us. Tami picked up her pace, but I broke into a full run. There was no bus in sight when I reached Aaron.

"Just kidding." He laughed at his joke. I didn't mind, except it felt like a blister was forming on my heel where the shoes slipped up and down. Tami scowled at him when she joined us, and then crossed the highway to wait inside the shelter Joel's grandfather had made for him.

Our stop was the last one on the route. Empty seats were scarce, so I plopped down in the first space I saw even though it meant sharing with Jolene. She smelled bad. Her family raised hogs and the distinctive hog-smell hung around her even though she looked clean. I smiled at her politely, and then fiddled with my book bag as if I were looking for something. A few minutes later the bus arrived at the school and I hurried off.

I found the door with Mrs. Pierce's name on it, the teacher Dad had chosen for me, but I stood outside the room and read the class roster, as if I didn't know to which teacher I'd been assigned. Only two new names marred the list of classmates I'd known all my life. I chewed on a strand of hair while I stalled outside the door. I never knew what to say the first time I saw someone, no matter how long I'd known them. I kept my eyes on the list, while kids crowded around looking for their name.

Suddenly Carol was beside me. "Roberta!" she squealed.

I squealed back. "Carol!"

"Oh, I love your dress!"

"Thanks." I wanted to add, "My mom made it," but that seemed like boasting and I didn't want to be rude. Instead I gushed, "I love your shoes!" It was easy to say. They were not saddle shoes.

Carol linked her arm in mine and we entered the classroom together. I felt myself smiling big, and couldn't stop. I didn't have a best friend like most of the girls from town did. We played tag or jumped rope or played games in groups, and while I was never left out, I didn't completely fit in. No one took me aside to share secrets or saved me a seat at lunch. Was this year going to be different?

Maybe Carol felt as awkward as I did. Ever since her dad died from cancer about three years ago, she'd had to help her mom in the café they owned next to the library. It probably didn't leave much time for making friends.

"Want to sit here?" she gestured to two seats, one in front of the other.

I nodded and put my book bag on top of the desk. Shelly waved from across the room and we waved back. Carol leaned close and whispered, "Is Shelly wearing lipstick?"

"Oh, my goodness! She is!" I forgot to whisper.

Shelly's lipstick wasn't the only change. Connie had cut off her waist-length hair; David was as tall as the teacher. Some things were the same. Sherrie Lou had just as many freckles; Sharon still wore her long, shiny, black hair in a pony tail wrapped with a beaded cord; Lona and Janie still laughed too loudly.

When the bell rang everyone took a seat. John, a dark-skinned boy from the reservation, sat in front of me. Across the aisle sat a new boy. He was tall, blond, and wore a green sweater over his plaid cotton shirt. When he saw me looking at him, he smiled and a tingly sensation shot through me. I smiled back, but my face felt hot and my hands got sweaty.

"Come to order, class." Mrs. Pierce stood in front looking firm and businesslike. She pulled her light blue cardigan close around her slim frame, and folded her arms waiting for us to settle down.

The PA crackled on and we stood for the Pledge of Allegiance and for a moment of silent prayer. The principal gave his usual welcome speech, then the PA crackled off. Mrs. Pierce cleared her throat.

"Welcome to the seventh grade." She pointed to her name already written on the board. "I am Mrs. Pierce. I look forward to being your teacher this year, but I must warn you, I expect you to pay attention and work hard." Her voice matched the sternness of the dark gray bun pulled tightly at the base of her neck. She eyed us over the top of her glasses. She might be short and thin, but there was nothing weak about the way she spoke or looked at us.

I recognized her from church, but then, every teacher I'd ever had was someone I could identify from somewhere in town. It made doing homework and obeying teachers necessary; you never knew when your parents might run into them at the post office or grocery store.

Mrs. Pierce's next words struck my heart. "You are old enough to know these are difficult times. To prepare for any eventuality, there will be a special drill this morning." She paused and returned to the middle of room. "An air raid drill. When the bell sounds, you will file out in pairs, into the hallway. Each of you will sit down, draw up your knees and lean over them. You will lock your hands over your heads and remain in that position until the bell sounds again."

She smoothed her dark blue dress with both hands and then continued. "This is different from the fire drills we have practiced in the past. You will not go outside. You will not talk; you will not run; you will not get out of line. The person to your right will be your partner for the exercise. You will make sure your partner walks out with you and gets in position."

I looked to my right at the new boy. My partner in an emergency was a boy—a boy whose name I didn't even know. Maybe he'd be willing to trade places with Carol. Later I'd ask her to ask him.

"Now let's get on with today's tasks. Frank, William, David, pass out the math books." She pointed to an overloaded table stacked with various textbooks. I took the math book given to me, signed the name plate, and recorded the book's condition. We did the same for the history, science, and reading texts. I practiced making a fancy capital *R* each time I wrote my name.

The new boy next to me dropped his pencil. It rolled near my foot, so I picked it up and handed it to him.

"Thanks." He smiled.

I smiled back, but couldn't say anything. *Oh, brother! Am I blushing?*

I felt a sharp poke from behind and turned to face Carol. She looked from me to the new boy and giggled. "He dropped it on purpose," she whispered.

Embarrassed I turned back to the front and kept my eyes down. Why did Carol say that? Had he heard her? *Was she right?*

The first day of school always dismissed early. We received our books for the year, signed them, attended the Welcome Back Assembly, then went home. As far as teachers were concerned, the first day of school was about distributing books and delivering mini-speeches. As far as the students were concerned, the first day of school was a chance to show off new clothes and see friends for the first time in three months.

The first day of a school year should not be about making a fool of yourself.

Chapter 21

Bombs Away!

I FINISHED WRITING MY NAME IN THE GRAMMAR BOOK JUST AS THE emergency bell rang. The new boy across from me jumped out of his chair, grabbed my hand, and pulled me toward the door. We held hands as we left the classroom and filed down the hallway. Then we sat, shoulder to shoulder, our backs against the wall. No one giggled; no one talked; the tension was as palpable as the green-painted walls.

I crouched on the floor, fear clutching my heart. This was too real; it brought the threat of bombs—nuclear bombs—too close. If danger was not imminent, we would not be practicing this drill on the first day of school—almost the first thing on the first day. What about my coat? How could my coat protect me if I wasn't wearing it? I didn't want to sit in a hallway with my head covered waiting for bombs to drop. I wanted someone to stop the bombs before they got here. No one had told us a plan for after the bombs come. *What if this isn't a drill, but the real thing and we haven't had time to practice?*

Mrs. Pierce walked down the hallway. Her sensible shoes made a sturdy clumping sound that was somehow reassuring. When the bell rang again, everyone stood up, but no one spoke. Somberly we filed back into the classroom and took our seats. Mrs. Pierce entered last. The door banged shut. I flinched.

The room was silent except for the clomping of Mrs. Pierce's shoes. As she neared her desk, an enormous boom rattled the windows. We all screamed, boys and girls alike, and dove under our desks. Even Mrs. Pierce dropped low to the floor. A second percussion followed closely behind the first. Someone screamed. Kids dashed to the cloak closet, some ran toward Mrs. Pierce. I crawled from under my desk and bolted for the door. I fumbled with the handle, and then tore down the deserted hallway. Bombs were dropping and my coat was at home; I wasn't going to sit in a hallway waiting for the roof to fall on me. A bell rang as I passed the administration office, but I didn't stop. I streaked through the exit doors and out to the sidewalk. Heedless of oncoming cars, I darted across the street, heading for the train tracks.

Old Joe was in the middle of the street. He wouldn't know anything about nuclear attacks or bomb threats! *Who will take care of Old Joe?* I needed to get home, needed to be safe at home, but I ran up to Old Joe and grabbed his arm.

"Come on, mister," I tearfully pleaded, tugging on his coat sleeve. "You've got to run, you've got to go." I yanked his arm, but he backed away as if I were crazy.

I turned and fled for my life. There was no light-colored coat to protect me. Speed was my only ally. I waited nervously as a dented, white pickup truck rambled through the blinking yellow light, and then I dashed across the street. I had to get home.

No one else ran along the sidewalk. No alarms rang; no sirens blared. No airplanes flew overhead. No police cars sped through the streets. *Why isn't everyone in town running for cover? Someone should tell them!* But I couldn't take time to warn anyone. Hadn't they heard the bombs?

I raced along the railroad tracks and down the lane, my breath coming in ragged heaves. Finally I scrambled up the front steps.

"Mom! Mom!" I looked wildly through the kitchen and living room.

I found her in the bathroom wearing her cleaning apron and smelling of Pine Sol. She wrapped me in her arms and spoke soothingly, reassuringly. The calmness of her voice, her comforting tone, her soft caresses calmed me. As my sobs decreased, I felt her take a deep breath. She walked me slowly to the sofa and sat beside me. For a minute she rested with her eyes closed, her lips moving silently. She took another deep breath. "What happened?" Her voice wavered slightly.

I felt her stiffen, bracing herself, waiting for my reply. "I need to know what happened," she repeated.

I hung my head. The panic had dissipated like steam from a tea kettle. What had happened? Mom was prepared for a tragedy, a crisis of monumental proportions. What had happened? Distant rumblings held the answer.

Fort Lewis was practicing maneuvers.

The phone rang and Mom got up to answer it. The kitchen door muffled her voice so I could not make out her words.

I saw her understanding smile as she returned to the couch, but I couldn't smile back; I was too embarrassed. I picked at a speck of lint on my sweater. "So, you've had some excitement this morning. Well, Fort Lewis rattled windows here too. Startled the socks off me. Are you hungry?"

I ate an apple, then plinked on the piano for a while before wandering outside. The artillery practice had ceased and the late morning was warm and pleasant, but I was restless. *What is happening now in the classroom? Is the whole school talking about me? I can't ever go back. I can never face anyone again, especially the new boy. Roberta, you are an idiot.* Every time I thought about the morning's events, heat flushed my face. I knew exactly how Anne felt after she smashed the slate over Gilbert's head and couldn't face returning to school.

Before long Tami and Aaron walked up the lane. I would know soon enough how much disgrace I had brought on myself. What had the kids on the bus said about my panicked exit?

I almost fled to the dogwoods, but I knew I would have to face Tami sometime. I sauntered to meet them as if there was nothing more natural than my being home ahead of them.

"Hey, there you are," shouted Aaron. "How did you get home already?"

I stopped cold. *He doesn't know how I got home. What else doesn't he know?* I shot a glance at Tami. She was fumbling with her books, not interested in how I got home or apparently anything else related to me.

"I, um, decided to walk."

No response from Tami.

"Guess what, Baby-Bertie. Tami's got a boyfriend," Aaron teased both of us with one sentence.

Tami shook her head. "What do you know about anything?"

"I saw you sitting with that tall geek at the assembly." Aaron sprinted away as he taunted, "Two little love birds sitting in a tree. K-I-S-S-I-N-G. First comes love, then comes marriage, then comes Tami with a baby carriage!"

Tami didn't chase after him, didn't threaten to get him later, didn't react to his childish taunt. I looked over at her. She shrugged and half smiled at me, a faraway look in her eyes. "Someday you'll understand," she said. "There's more to life than books and make-believe, you know." She walked ahead of me, a light spring to her step.

I did understand: she was talking about boys. That dreamy, wistful look? I understood that too. I wouldn't have yesterday, or even when school began this morning, but I'd had a hint today and it was enough. A new awareness had awakened in me and even though I looked the same, I knew I was different. It was too new to talk about, too private to share.

I also understood why I wasn't being teased. The bell I had heard as I pushed through the school doors had called everyone to the Welcome Assembly. In the chaos before the bell, no one saw what I'd done.

At least that's what I hoped. Neither Aaron nor Tami had heard anything, but someone in my class had missed me or Mom wouldn't have gotten a phone call. Mrs. Pierce?

The next morning I chewed on a strand of hair as I entered the school. None of the kids on the bus had smirked at me, no one in the hallway pointed or whispered, but I hesitated at the door of the classroom before walking quickly to my seat. I made eye contact with no one until the PA signaled for the Pledge. As I stood, the new boy glanced my way a few times, but he wasn't acting as if I was weird. When our eyes met, he winked at me. I blushed and quickly looked away but I couldn't hold back a smile. In math, we passed our papers to the right to check them. Mrs. Pierce read the answers and then said, "Sign your name to the paper you corrected and pass it forward."

I wrote Roberta with a fancy *R* right under the name *Raul*. Heat rushed up my neck as I looked at the two names together.

After school I hurried to my secret garden. None of my fears from the day before had happened, but I'd learned a lesson. This had been a narrow escape. Fear had almost made a complete fool of me. It wouldn't happen again. I thought about Daniel in the lion's den, Aaron's favorite Bible story. Not every scary situation had to be controlled by fear. What about Marguerite? Didn't she throw fear aside to try to warn her Scarlet Pimpernel? I spoke my resolve aloud to the trees, as if the mighty pillars could hold me responsible for my words.

"I declare this day that fear will never again control me. I will never panic. I am not afraid."

I stood tall, my back straight, head up, eyes focused on the towering trees. I felt like Marguerite, like Daniel, like Harriet Tubman and Joan of Arc. I thought deciding not to give way to fear would be enough to conquer it.

I was wrong.

Chapter 22

The Storm

"KHRUSHCHEV DENIES OFFENSIVE WEAPONS IN CUBA," RAN THE headline. As Dad read the article aloud at the dinner table, my body stiffened. Every day it was the same debate: Cuba has missiles. Cuba doesn't have missiles. Cuba has only defensive missiles. The Soviets deny a weapons buildup. The French claim the Soviets are lying.

Dad read on. My feet tapped the floor; I chased a pea around my plate with my fork. My mouth was silent, but in my head I sang loudly, trying to drown out Dad's voice, *I've been working on the railroad all the live-long day. I've been working on the railroad just to pass the time away . . .*

Mom's voice grabbed my attention. "I wish we had a plan, Ron. Some emergency plan. Just in case."

Dad nodded at Mom's request. *Should I show him what I've done in the storeroom?* I chewed on my braid. Later. I'd show him later when no one else was around. Maybe he'd be proud of me, but he might be angry that I'd gone behind his back.

When his car rumbled down the lane before dark on Columbus Day, I knew it meant trouble and I hadn't shown him the storeroom yet or heard a word about his plan. The Studebaker lurched to a stop on the back side of the detached garage, a place he never parked. Aaron and I raced our bikes toward him. *Tell us the plan, Dad! What's the plan?* The words jostled in my head; he spoke before I got them out of my mouth. "Put your bikes in the toolshed." *That's the plan against nuclear attack? Saving our bikes in the toolshed?*

He moved the station wagon into the garage and barred the double wooden doors. *Shouldn't we be getting in the car? Shouldn't we go far, far away?* He turned, surveying the land around, and then strode to his shop and emerged with a coiled rope. *Show him the storeroom! Tell him!*

"Aaron, over here!" They headed toward the pasture where two friendly, red Herefords and one ornery Black Angus grazed. I waited near the toolshed, fighting the panic with slow, deep breaths. A blackbird cawed. I spied him perched high in a fir tree. Looking at the tree reminded me of my promise. Fear would not control me. When Dad returned, I'd show him the preparations I'd made in the storeroom.

Soon Aaron came back up the hill, a switch in his hand and the two Herefords moseying along in front of him. He opened a rickety gate that led into a small enclosure with a cinder-block shed. Dad used the hut with its grassy corral to doctor ailing animals. Two strands of electric wire separated the shed and small pen from the rest of the pasture.

Moo. Moo. I could hear the Angus bawling as Dad worked his way up the hill.

"Dagnabit!" Dad swore, and I knew the steer was giving him trouble again. He came into sight, pulling and dragging the animal by a rope around its neck. Progress came in inches.

"Aaron," he yelled. "Open the gate and stand ready in case this blamed thing bolts."

The gate was narrow and the Herefords grazed near it. Aaron

shooed them into a corner, and then opened the gate and stood beside it, forcing the obstinate Black Angus to take the path into the pen. The steer's neck stretched out as Dad tugged on the lead. Its large brown eyes bulged. It snorted and bawled and fought against the line. Slowly Dad pulled it inside the gate, but suddenly the Angus bolted forward, the rope slackened, and Dad lost his balance. The steer charged into the electric fence and went crazy. Its horns tangled in the wire. Dad heaved on the rope, digging in his heels, but the beast was uncontrollable. It bucked and twisted and bawled.

The Herefords startled from their corner and bellowed. Aaron slammed the gate closed and started to climb over it, but Dad yelled at him to stay on the other side. The enraged steer twisted and writhed, destroying the enclosure with its lunging and bucking.

Dad yelled, "Roberta! Run! Turn off the fence!"

I stood paralyzed by the noise and chaos. He yelled again, "Go! Now!"

I ran, but I didn't know where to go. *How do I turn off the fence? Where is the switch to the fence? Think, Roberta! Maybe the fuse box in the shop? But I wasn't ever to touch a fuse box! Where else? But it had to be at the fuse box. What if I'm wrong?* I ran to the box on the wall and looked at the confusing rows of glass fuses. None of them were labeled and none of them had a switch. I stared at a lever at the top of the box. Was that the switch?

What do I do? What do I do? I did nothing, afraid of pulling the lever, afraid of touching the fuses. The cattle bellowed. Aaron screeched something over and over. My brain screamed, *Do something!* Still I stood there, staring at the box, at the wires, afraid to move, afraid that whatever I did would be the wrong thing. I felt like a deer caught in headlights, staring at danger without sense enough to act.

Aaron pushed past me. "Get outta the way!" He jumped up on

a wooden crate to reach the lever, pulled it down, and then rushed back to the corral. Mom and Tami raced from the house. They didn't see me standing in the darkened shop, but rushed past. "Ron! Ron!" Mom cried as she ran.

Timidly I joined my family outside the demolished pen. The Herefords had quieted. The uneasy Black Angus snorted and pawed the ground. Dad tied the head rope to a sturdy fence post. In a flash he roped a back foot and tied it off so the steer couldn't move. As he cut away the mass of wire, he snapped orders: "All of you, hustle! Fill empty jars with water, the bathtub too. Stack the woodbox full. Get candles and matches."

Each of us sped away, charged by the urgency in Dad's voice. No one asked why; not even Mom stopped to question his instructions. Aaron carried in load after load of wood; Tami filled jars and the bathtub with water. Mom and I gathered candles, matches, batteries, flashlights, and a first aid kit. This was good. With all the supplies gathered, taking them to the storeroom would be easy. No bomb blasts had rattled the windows; there was still time. *Will Dad forgive me for not turning off the fence when he sees the storeroom?*

Dad joined us in the kitchen, red-faced and breathing hard. He took out his white handkerchief and wiped sweat and blood from his face. His shirt sleeve was torn revealing nasty scrapes and gouges; a trickle of red oozed down his arm. He sat in the chair and Mom dabbed at his wounds with a washcloth. Tami set the iodine on the table. I couldn't look—not at his wounds, nor at Mom tending them, and especially not in his eyes, but I needed to tell him about the storeroom-turned-bomb-shelter. I took a deep breath.

"Well, Ron?" Mom spoke first as she dabbed iodine on his scratches.

"The cattle are fine; locked in the shed."

"That's not what I want to know." Her voice was low and husky.

"It's a hurricane. A hurricane is coming."

"But we don't get hurricanes."

That's it? A hurricane? I wanted to dance and clap my hands. People survived hurricanes all the time. No one survives nuclear bombs.

"Doug was returning from a meeting in Portland, had his car radio set to a local station. Portland radio began broadcasting a hurricane warning around 10:30 this morning. They're saying Hurricane Freda is headed for the West Coast."

"Portland radio? What about Seattle radio?" Disbelief showed in Mom's voice.

"I don't know. A lot of people will be caught off guard. Some of the guys in the office didn't believe Doug. They scoffed at the idea of a hurricane striking Washington or Oregon. But Doug said all the Portland radio stations are alerting residents to prepare for the worse storm in West Coast history. I checked the barometer. Then I came home."

"What about my mother and Marge? Do they know?" Mom headed for the phone.

"On my way here I stopped at the tavern and told Dan. He called your mother right then."

Mom returned to dabbing iodine on Dad's scrapes. "Maybe we should pray now before it gets here," she whispered. Dad turned in his chair as Mom sank to her knees in front of him. He enveloped her small hands in his thick ones and the room grew silent. No one spoke, no one prayed in high and lofty tones or even whispered. There was just Mom and Dad holding hands, eyes closed, heads bowed, and silence.

We watched from the front porch as the sky turned an eerie color, a hue I had never seen. The wind began gently, and then whipped and gusted as it gathered strength. Two gigantic fir trees near the house creaked and groaned as small branches broke off and flew away. The brown grass in the pasture lay flat. As the intensity increased, the roar of the wind filled our ears. Uprooted shrubs bounced in the pasture like popcorn over a campfire. A gust whooshed across the porch and I grabbed hold of a sturdy square pillar holding up the roof; Aaron held on to Dad.

We retreated to the back porch, where the wind knocked against the door and bullied the windows, but could not get in. The sky darkened and the hurricane's power increased. When the lights flickered, then went out, we put lit candles in every room where their flames sputtered and danced. Mom moved the stew from the gas stove to the trash burner which produced enough heat to warm the kitchen. An occasional downdraft caused puffs of smoke to escape through cracks in the small wood stove and the kitchen smelled wonderfully of beef stew and wood smoke.

I felt like I did at the seashore. The blasts of wind evoked the same thrill as the pounding, crashing waves of a churning sea. Oh! How I'd like to see the ocean now, with this storm upon it! The windows rattled as creaks and crashes, thuds and thumps increased. We moved to the living room and Mom closed the new, heavy drapes while Dad lit a kerosene lamp. We huddled near each other, wrapped in blankets, listening to the wind whine and roar while unknown objects bumped and banged in the dark.

Crack! At the thunderous sound, we rushed to the windows. The tops of two giant fir trees crashed down and fell across the lane.

I stared at the frantically whipping trees. These were not friendly swaying branches! Huge limbs snapped off as if they were matchsticks. A doghouse from some neighbor rolled over and over as if it were a beach ball. This was not a playful storm; this was a monster!

My breath came fast and shallow. My eyes stung. *I'm afraid; I'm afraid; I'm afraid.* The words chased each other in my head.

I looked at Dad and Mom, standing together, their arms around each other. Dad's eyes were bright—fear or excitement? But his forehead was not wrinkled in worry lines. His mouth was not drawn tight. Mom's face looked calm, her eyes clear.

Dad walked over to the bookshelf. "Tamara, will you read to us?"

He handed her a Bible and she immediately turned to a passage. "God is our refuge and strength, an ever-present help in trouble. Therefore we will not fear, though the earth give way and the mountains fall into the heart of the sea . . ."

The fearful words bouncing in my head faded. I closed my eyes and snuggled on the couch in my blanket, listening to Tami's voice. Aaron cuddled beside me.

A thunderous crash shook the house. Tami stopped reading. Aaron's body stiffened. Dad stood up. "I'll be right back." He went into the hallway, came back, and disappeared behind the kitchen door.

"Will you read a story, Tami? Maybe about Daniel?"

Good idea, Aaron.

Chapter 23

Aftermath

I FELL ASLEEP CURLED ON THE LIVING ROOM FLOOR, WRAPPED IN A warm quilt listening to Tami read; I awoke in my bed. There was no sound: no wind, no early morning stirrings. I snuggled deeper under my covers, straining my ears for clues. *Am I the only one awake?* Aaron's bed was empty. I shoved my feet into my slippers, wrapped my bathrobe around me and shuffled to the kitchen.

Mom and Dad were drinking coffee; Aaron had a mug of hot chocolate. The trash burner warmed the kitchen, but there was no electricity, therefore no lights, no television, no water. The kitchen window revealed debris flung everywhere: tree branches of every size, shingles, buckets, and fence posts. I blushed at the sight of blue jeans wrapped around the oak tree. I'd forgotten about throwing our muddy clothes out the storeroom window after digging for dinosaur bones. Had Mom seen them?

Dad drained his cup of coffee and stood, dressed in his logging clothes. "Gonna assess the damage."

"May I come?" Aaron looked ready for an adventure. Dad hesitated, then nodded.

Mom scooted her chair back. "Let's all go. There's not much I can do inside without electricity, and I'd like to see what this storm has done."

I hurried into Aaron's room to grab my clothes, then spotted Tami through her open door. She sat on the edge of her bed rubbing sleep from her eyes. "Hey, we're all going outside to see the damage. Come on. Get dressed." I rushed to the bathroom with my jeans and sweatshirt. Tami stood outside the door. "Hurry!" she rasped in a not-quite-awake voice. "I gotta go!"

The first place we explored was the mammoth heap of treetops. Aaron raced ahead and leaped onto a thick log. Then he yelled and jumped back down, his arms waving wildly as if he were trying to swish away a horde of insects. He was.

"Run!" Dad shouted. Mom grabbed my hand, and Dad dragged Aaron along as a swarm of bees chased us back to the house.

Aaron got stung a couple of times, but he didn't cry. Mom put a baking soda plaster on each sting, and then produced a deck of cards from the cupboard. We played rummy until Dad got fidgety. When he went outside, the rest of us remained behind. Who knew what other dangers the storm had created?

When Dad returned, his eyes met Mom's and the look they exchanged told me everything was okay; the world was right again.

Aaron and I zipped up our play coats and bounced outdoors, tired of a house without electricity. We skirted the mangled treetops, and headed for the field where we had built our fort. The little trees surrounding it had been limber enough to bend without breaking; none of them were harmed, but the hurricane had destroyed our fort. The fence posts from the walls were strewn throughout the meadow.

The wind had betrayed me. It made magnificent ocean swells; it made the trees wave friendly howdy-dos and the tall grass ripple. It wasn't supposed to be treacherous; it wasn't supposed to tear apart and destroy. I chewed on a strand of hair. Who could stop wind? Wind could happen any time. Maybe a big wind was gathering strength even now. Perhaps another hurricane was headed our way and we didn't know it. I searched the tops of the trees for a clue and shivered at their faint movement.

We walked on without talking. Aaron pointed to a huge toppled tree, its root wad taller than Dad. We neared the migrant workers' housing, but nothing remained of my old playhouse except scattered piles of debris. Not a single wall stood.

An urgent need to check on my garden overwhelmed me—but I needed to do it alone; I couldn't share this secret place with anyone. I glanced sideways at Aaron. *How do I get rid of him?*

A slight breeze brushed my face and ruffled my hair. I checked the sky to see if it was turning the eerie color of the evening before, but it remained clear and blue. I kicked at a burnt board and sniffed, then thrust my hands in my pockets and paced back and forth near a tangled mass of splintered boards. The air smelled of smoke and ash.

"Want to go back home?" I didn't look at Aaron, but he heard me.

"Guess so."

"Then go."

"What? I thought you wanted to go home?" Aaron's voice was testy.

"I didn't say I wanted to go home. I asked if you wanted to go home." I was testy back.

I turned away from him and kicked at a dirt clod. The ache to see my garden grew. I needed to know if the storm had damaged my dogwood trees. I hadn't gone back inside my playhouse since Dad ordered me not to, but it had still been there. Now it wasn't even a heap of boards. It felt as if a part of me were missing. What if my garden was destroyed too?

I pivoted to face Aaron. "You're such a baby!" I sneered and stomped up the hill to the maple tree. My words were mean and undeserved, but with each stomp my anger deepened and I looked for something—for someone—to lash out at. I slumped down on the swing, the swing that had taken me into the heavens, the swing where the rhythmic up and down motion had quelled my unrest. I pumped back and forth, my emotion rising, faster and furiously.

Downcast, Aaron trudged on. As he neared me, I kicked at him. I didn't want to hit him, I just wanted to kick *at* something. The energetic movement unbalanced the swing and it twisted in the air, on a crooked angle. I quit pumping to let it straighten out.

Aaron acted as if he didn't see what I'd done. He retreated home and I wound the thick ropes around each other until they were twisted tightly. When I lifted my feet, I whirled in ever-faster circles, spinning, spinning, spinning. It brought me no joy.

The swing stopped. I slid off and pushed it away, but I didn't move fast enough and with its return, the wooden seat bumped against my leg. It didn't hurt, but my anger was overpowering. The swing was my enemy. I wanted to damage it. I wanted it to feel pain. I pummeled it with my hands, but that hurt, so I kicked it. The swing jerked this way and that, unpredictable and erratic. I kicked and missed. I called it names. "This is a little silly," a voice in my head nagged. "So what!" I argued back. Then I remembered my garden again.

Under the wire, through the berry thicket, into the heart of the garden I crept. The summer ferns were brown and dead, but the moss was green and thick. Broken limbs littered the ground, but the trees were intact. My precious dogwoods suffered no broken tops, nor had they been stripped of any big branches. The garden was safe!

I leaned against a tree and gazed up to the heights of surrounding evergreens; my anger ebbed. The cedar tree behind the dogwood had lost its top in the storm. A breeze whispered through its branches and they waved a friendly reply. It was a harmless zephyr, but it caught a weakened branch. The branch whisked free and rode the wind to the ground. It didn't come near me, but I was uneasy. Everywhere I looked, branches rocked back and forth. *Are the waves friendly? Is this a harmless breeze or the beginning of a hurricane? How can I know?*

The tops of mighty evergreens swayed in the wind and I couldn't get away from them. What if more branches were loose and ready to break? What if broken branches were dislodged by the wind? What if the swaying trees crashed down? I could not take my eyes off the treetops, nor control my fear. Branches creaked and groaned. Tears welled up and spilled over.

Is there nowhere safe in this world? How many times had I viewed this game played by wind and trees and been a part of it? How many times had I lain on my back and watched these very trees dance in the wind and felt their exuberance? I sobbed as limbs scratched against each other. Every puff of wind set my heart fluttering. Where was my brother? If I had let Aaron come with me, we could run away together the same way we had fled the bees.

I didn't want to be alone: not alone with the fuse box, not alone on the swing, not alone in my garden. I closed my eyes and imagined Aaron racing down the knoll, calling my name. When I opened my eyes, I was still by myself.

Bursts of sound filtered to me. *What is that? People noises? Is someone screaming? Laughing?* Fear's hold loosened as I headed toward the sounds. By the time I reached the swing I heard my family laughing. I walked closer.

Mom, Dad, Aaron, and Tami were cleaning up the yard. As Dad turned his back and bent over to pick up a handful of debris, Mom tossed a twig, hitting him lightly on his backside. Dad straightened up, turned around, and pointed accusingly at Aaron. Mom and Tami broke into fits of laughter. They pointed at each other, hooting loudly.

I couldn't see Dad's face; he was turned away from me. Was he angry? Was he smiling? I stepped closer and Mom saw me. Her eyes were bright, her face flushed. She nodded slightly and when Dad bent over again, they rushed him.

"Dog pile on Dad!" Aaron shouted. Mom tackled Dad first. Tami and Aaron jumped together. I ached to jump too, but was it all right? Would Dad be mad at all of us? I ran close, but stopped short of leaping on the pile. *Is it okay?*

Aaron lifted his head. "Come on, Bertie!"

I jumped on top. The pile began to move. From its bottom came violent rolling and shaking. Laughing, Aaron fell off and took me with him. Tami rolled off; only Mom hung on tight. Mom giggled and hung onto Dad's back as he twisted and turned underneath her. And then an amazing sound: Dad laughed! I wanted the moment to last forever.

Mom and Dad got up and we all worked at undoing the storm's mess. The four of them teased one another as they worked. I wanted to play too, but I didn't know how. I could get away with throwing a stick in Tami's hair or tackling Aaron when he bent over, but I wanted to tease Dad and make him laugh.

I didn't know the rules for this game; we hadn't played it before. I watched Tami try to stuff leaves down Dad's shirt, but she was short and he was tall, and she failed miserably. Instead, Dad chased her with his own handful of leaves. The leaves showered down on her, some sticking in her hair, some balancing on her shoulders. I wished it was me Dad chased, that it was me with leaves tumbling down on my head.

We slept in on Sunday morning. The power was still out in town, so Sunday school was cancelled, but the church was packed for the worship service. Dad said there were more people than on Christmas and Easter. Some of the people forgot the "no talking in the sanctuary" rule and a low buzz of conversation continued until the acolytes walked down the aisle ready to light the altar candles.

"Why isn't the organ playing?" Aaron whispered to Dad.

"No electricity," Dad whispered back.

Pastor Hoyer asked us to rise for a prayer. When we sat back down, a deep, sonorous voice reverberated from the choir loft. "Our Father which art in heaven. Hallowed be Thy name . . ." The song was slow and deep and powerful.

I knew it was Mr. Swansen singing even though I couldn't see him. I closed my eyes and nothing existed in the world except this amazing sound. It was as if the voice itself crept into my very core. The voice swelled with the final phrases, filling the sanctuary with power and hope. "For Thine is the kingdom and the power and the glory for ever."

I thought my heart would stop; I couldn't breathe. I opened my eyes as this single voice, unaccompanied by the organist, carried me up, up, up to the stained glass window behind the wooden cross. The colors and the voice mixed together and I *became* color and music. I never wanted it to stop.

"For ever. And ever. And ever." The most thunderous and deepest tones yet.

Then ever so soft: "Amen."

Chapter 24

Ridiculous

AFTER THREE DAYS WITHOUT POWER, MRS. SWANSEN SAID IT WAS A sign from God that the last days were upon us. She said it was His punishment for the wickedness of the people. Dad said it was a sign that the power company was understaffed and inefficient.

Monday morning, Dad left for his office in Tacoma; the rest of us worked outside. Mom raked leaves, while Tami and I piled limbs on burn piles and Aaron climbed the oak tree to remove a battered metal bucket.

"Just toss it on the garbage heap, Aaron." Mom rarely discarded anything. Something about "waste not, want not," but there was no salvaging broken buckets and tangled strands of barbed wire.

After lunch it rained. Aaron built forts with Lincoln Logs. Tami and I worked on a jigsaw puzzle Mom had spread out on a card table in the living room close to the front window. After a while I tired of looking for impossible-to-find pieces—why did they make the sky the same color as the water? I sat down at the piano. I disliked "When Butterflies Blink Their Primrose Wings," but Mrs. Dempsey wouldn't let me move on to anything more interesting until a gold star topped the page.

I pretended that butterflies with rose-colored wings had been captured by Communists intent on destroying them and all things beautiful. If I played the first page perfectly, they had to let the butterflies free. Carefully I plunked out the tune, but hit two wrong notes in the last measure. *That was just practice.* I tried again from the beginning but missed the first F-sharp.

I changed the rules. For each note perfectly played, a butterfly would be freed.

I messed up the whole first measure. "That was just for practice, not for real." I didn't mean to speak out loud, but Aaron heard me.

"If it isn't for real, can you play just for pretend?"

"Yeah, pretend play so we don't have to pretend we can't hear you." Tami laughed at her own joke.

I left the piano and searched the bookshelf for my old fairy-tale book. With Grandma Benson's afghan wrapped tightly around me, I curled up on the couch, and read the inscription on the inside cover for the umpteenth time: *To Roberta, with love from Mom and Dad, Christmas 1956.* A long, long time ago, Mom used to read it aloud almost every night. Suddenly I wanted her to read to me again. I wanted her to sit on the couch with Tami on one side, me on the other, and Aaron in her lap, the pages turned to "Puss in Boots." *If I ask her will she read now?* I looked at Mom and Tami hovering over the puzzle. Tami saw me watching them.

"So, fairy tales? Really, Bertie. What will Jane and Elizabeth think?"

I wanted to say, "Jane and Elizabeth would think you are *despicable*," but I ignored her, pulled the afghan closer and turned to page three. I read until Mom called me to set the table for dinner.

After the dishes were done, we all five played progressive rummy at the kitchen table by the light of a kerosene lantern. I liked the games because there were rules. I understood the rules and followed them. I wasn't nervous about what to do or not do. Sometimes I kept the wrong card, but no one knew it except me. Sometimes I even won. Three days without power did not feel to me like God's judgment on the world.

On the evening of the fourth day everything changed.

As usual, Dad read the front page news out loud at the dinner table. "A U-2 reconnaissance aircraft has secured definitive evidence of several SS-4 nuclear missiles in Cuba. The discovery contradicts Soviet claims that they have no plans to arm Cuba with nuclear weapons."

"Roberta, get your hair out of your mouth." *Didn't Mom hear what Dad read? Why is she more concerned about my hair than missiles in Cuba? Why doesn't she say, "Russia, get your missiles out of Cuba"?*

"Maybe Mrs. Swansen is right about the end of the world." I don't think Tami meant to say it out loud, but it didn't matter, because maybe it *was* the end of the world.

As Tami and I cleared the table, Mom and Dad went into their room. I heard their door shut, but minutes later, Dad reentered the kitchen. "Leave the dishes, girls. We're going to Grandma's."

Leave the dishes? Going to Grandma Benson's on a weeknight after dinner? The newness of it alarmed me. Never had we gone somewhere with dirty dishes in the sink. We went to Grandma's after church on a Sunday or for a picnic in the summer, but never after dinner on a weeknight. I put on my light-colored coat before getting in the car.

Normally the ride took about fifteen or twenty minutes, but detours around blocked roads lengthened the trip. All the while, the car radio blasted news about Cuba, Soviets, President Kennedy, and something called the "Joint Chiefs of Staff." They even brought up the "Bay of Pigs fiasco." I tried singing loudly in my head to drown out the newscast, but it didn't work. I plugged my ears and watched trees lining the road zip by.

Aaron nudged me, then tapped his finger on a picture in his latest library book. The drawing was a skeleton of a something-asaurus; Aaron pointed to its skull and jawbone. With a little imagination, it resembled the cow skull we had found in the swamp.

Just what I needed, a reminder of failure to match the mounting fear. "Leave me alone," I snapped. As soon as I said it, I was sorry, but I didn't tell him.

The past several days had been fun, working together outside, playing games as a family, no television news to disrupt the evening. I'd let down my guard and I was paying for it now. It felt like fear had taken a minivacation, but returned with a carload of friends. I sucked on my hair and sniffed back tears. What if the bombs came while we were on this detour and we couldn't find shelter? I glanced at my brother in his dark brown jacket and Tami beside him in her dark blue one. I should have told them the secret about light colors.

We parked in front of Grandma's house and she greeted us at the door, wiping her hands on an apron. "Well, if this isn't a surprise! Come on in." She held open the door.

Aaron and I didn't race for the cookie jar; Tami didn't request a measurement. We removed our coats and surrounded the wood cookstove that Grandma still used. A hint of wood smoke and homemade bread teased the air.

Dad didn't waste any time. "Have you heard the news?"

Grandma nodded.

"We've talked about converting your cellar into a shelter; I think we'd better do it."

When did we talk about making a shelter for Grandma?

Grandma nodded again. "Been thinking the same thing."

What about us? We need one, too!

I spat my braid from my mouth. I wanted to confront Dad and demand he answer the questions battering in my head. *What about us, Dad? Let Grandpa Benson fix up their own stupid old cellar. How about you fix up our storeroom?* If the anger I felt showed on my face, Dad might have hauled me to the woodshed, but he didn't look at me.

"Grandpa will be back in a minute. Let's us have a look-see now." Grandma handed Dad and Mom a flashlight and they went downstairs into the cellar. When Tami and Aaron followed them, I hurried to catch up.

The three flashlights brightened the square, windowless basement. The only other exit was through a trap door over the coal bin. Plywood shelves lined one concrete wall and, as in our storeroom, the shelves were crowded with jars of fruits and vegetables. Barrels nearby were heaped with potatoes, onions, and apples. I expected the room to be full of spiders and mice droppings, like our storeroom, but I should have known better. Grandma wouldn't let a mouse or spider in her spotless house, not even under it.

She walked to the middle of the room. "You've got that old chrome table you could bring over and I've got some chairs in the attic."

Why should Grandma get my table? We need it! Is she going to take the couch and chifforobe too? I couldn't stay to hear more. I eased up the stairs, but as I rounded the corner into the kitchen, I bumped into Grandpa Benson.

"Oomph!" He stepped back.

"Excuse me, sir!" I zipped around him, into the kitchen, and outside. Light from a kerosene lantern on the table shone through the window, making a patch of yellow on the lawn. Shadows lurked along the fence. *What is that black clump against the house? Did it move?* I started to go back inside, but through the window I saw Grandpa Benson putting a piece of wood in the stove. Danger outside, danger inside. Would Dad come running if he heard me screaming? Could he hear me? *Settle down, Roberta. It's just a shadow.*

A breeze came up off the lake and I shivered. The black clump shivered too. My brain screamed, but my tight throat silenced the sound. I'd have run to the kitchen, Grandpa Benson or not, but my feet wouldn't move. Had the mysterious clump seen me? Was it watching me now? Why was it lurking against the house? *What is it?*

"I'm not afraid. I'm not afraid." I whispered the words to myself. Hadn't I vowed never to let fear rule me again? *Come on, Roberta, just go in the house. One foot in front of the other. Go in the house.* My feet felt as if they were cemented to the sidewalk.

A fallen limb, about the size of a baseball bat lay beside the walkway. The thought of a potential weapon empowered me. Anger ate the fear, propelling me into action.

I knelt as if to tie my shoe, spat the hair from my mouth, and took a deep breath. I grabbed the piece of wood and raced toward the menacing black thing, brandishing my weapon and screaming, "Aaaaaaaaaah! Get out of here! Aaaaaaaaah!" I didn't intend to hit anything, just scare whatever it was away, but I tripped over debris left in the yard by the storm. I hurled forward, hit against the house, and landed smack on top of the dark mass.

Grandpa Benson tapped on the window in the kitchen door, then folded his arms across his chest.

Oh, Roberta, what did you do?

The door squeaked open; Grandpa stepped outside. I struggled up off Grandma's favorite hydrangea bush, its middle broken and flattened to the ground. "Meant to prune that bush a couple weeks ago." The door shut and he was gone.

Whoa. I caught my breath. Grandpa Benson just saw me do a stupid thing and he didn't yell. Yell? He actually spoke civilly. I dropped the club and leaned against the house. I'd given Grandpa a good reason to haul me off to his woodshed, and instead of cursing at me, he spoke, well, *amicably.*

The whole scene felt as if I'd dreamed it. Did I? Was this a fantasy gone wrong? Was I like Old Joe, unable to distinguish reality from make-believe? No, a smattering of bruises and scratches assured me I hadn't been dreaming.

As Dad drove home, words bounced in my head and emotions flitted through my heart. I tried to sort them out, but nothing made sense. Fear still controlled me. When I tried to act against it, I did stupid things, like beating hydrangea bushes.

The dirty Commies lied and Cuba has missiles. Dad wants to prepare a bomb shelter for Grandma, but not for us. I sniffed and Dad glanced back at me. "Get your hair out of your mouth, Roberta."

I'd been terrified in the dark. Then angry. I didn't know that much anger lived inside me. I shuddered.

Grandpa Benson didn't yell. That was big. What did it mean? I felt my face redden at the thought of my attack on the bush while he watched. How funny it must have looked to him. I imagined headlines in the paper. "Girl Attacks Hydrangea Bush to Save Family." I chuckled out loud.

"What's so funny, Bertie?"

"Oh, Aaron, I did the most ridiculous thing outside at Grandma's." I grinned at my brother bundled in his dark brown coat, and my smile evaporated. My throat tightened and my body tensed, as I realized I'd done a second ridiculous thing, a dangerous thing, a not-funny thing.

I'd forgotten my coat at Grandma's.

Chapter 25

Breaking Rules

On Thursday the front page news focused on U.S. bombs. "An airdrop test over the Johnston Island area was conducted today."

Why are we testing bombs? Are we planning to use them? Don't we know if they work? The uncertainty about U.S. bombs added a layer of fear. What if the dirty Commies attacked, and we couldn't do anything because our testing wasn't done? What if we were testing so we could attack first?

I risked talking to Tami about it while we did the dinner dishes. "Do you know where Johnston Island is?"

"Nope."

Through the window above the sink I watched Aaron play stage-coach driver on the wood box. I wished make-believe would zap the fear like it used to. But even if it would, I didn't want to play his game. I didn't want to shoot anybody, and I didn't want anyone shooting at me. Not even pretend.

"Tami, what are we going to do?"

"Finish the dishes."

"That's not what I mean." I stopped drying the blue bowl and faced her.

She turned to me. "We are going to finish the dishes, then you are going to lose at the card game tonight, because I feel like winning, and then we're going to bed." She went back to scrubbing the pot.

The evening went as she predicted, except that we ate popcorn as we played the game that she won.

When bedtime came, I put on my nightgown in the bathroom as usual, but I didn't go to my bed in Aaron's room right away. I wanted to talk to Tami more. I wanted to know why she was not afraid, but her door was closed and I couldn't make myself turn the knob. My flashlight beam traced the door frame while I fought for courage to enter the room in which Oma died. Aaron saw me standing there. "Bertie! Flashlight Face!"

I spun at the sound of my name; his flashlight beam hit me full in the face.

Red spots danced in front of my eyes. "I wasn't ready. Do it again?"

It was a game we'd played since Dad gave us the lights a day after the storm. Aaron stood at one end of the hall and I stood at the other, our backs turned to each other.

"Flashlights, off!" We spoke the command together.

Aaron counted. "One, two, three!"

On "three" we spun to face each other and switched on our lights. The first one to shine his light in the other's face was the winner. It was a silly game, but I liked it anyway. It was part of the fun of no electricity.

Mom came to tuck us in bed. "Are you two wasting batteries?"

"No, we're having fun."

Mom ruffled Aaron's hair. "Get in bed. And keep your lights off unless you *need* them."

Friday's front-page story brought a surprise and with it, hope. "Yesterday President Kennedy met with Soviet Foreign Minister

Andrei Gromyko. Gromyko denied the presence of Soviet weapons in Cuba stating that 'all military activity is of a defensive nature.'"

This Andrei person was a minister; he'd tell the truth. He'd have to because ministers were *righteous*. Our minister would never lie; he preached against it. If a minister said something was true, even if he was a *foreign minister*, you could believe it, couldn't you? Finally positive news from someone we could trust.

But Dad rustled us from bed early on Saturday. "Get dressed and get in the car."

Sleepy-eyed I crawled in the car with everyone else. We hadn't eaten breakfast; neither Aaron nor I had made our beds or done any chores. Why were we breaking rules? What did it mean? I sucked on a strand of uncombed hair.

In a short while we parked in front of Auntie Marge's. She had breakfast waiting on the table, but I didn't want sausage and hash browns and eggs. I wanted the Saturday breakfast Dad always made. I wanted *his* pancakes, with *his* brown sugar syrup. He didn't need electricity for that; he'd done it on the little wood stove before. We didn't have to come to Auntie Marge's for breakfast. So why had we?

After we ate, Dad hauled a white bed sheet bulging with dirty clothes from the back of the car into my aunt's laundry room. Mom filled the washing machine with jeans and sweatshirts. "When did your power come back on?" She sounded a little jealous.

Tami came into the kitchen, her wet hair done up in a towel. "Your turn, Bertie."

"My turn for what?"

"A bath."

I soaked in Auntie Marge's deep tub full of bubbles and took a long time washing my hair. It felt safe in the bathroom, all steamy and small and quiet. I didn't know what was happening on the other side of the door. I wanted to know, but I was scared by the broken rules. I understood taking a bath here, where we didn't have to heat water on the stove, but what about not making our beds or not having Saturday breakfast? I couldn't remember a time when anyone left our house with an unmade bed. It just never happened.

After I got dressed, I found Aaron watching cartoons on the color TV and eating candy from the pretty glass dish Auntie Marge kept on an end table. The house was quiet except for the television.

"Aaron." I waited for him to look at me. "Where is everyone?"

"Gone to Grandma Benson's." He turned back to the cartoon.

"Why? Why did they leave us here?"

"I don't know. Hey, have you ever seen cartoons in color? Did you know Road Runner is blue? I thought he was red."

I watched Wile E. Coyote fall off a cliff while Road Runner beep-beeped on the road below. Then I wandered into the kitchen where my aunt was putting biscuits into a basket lined with a yellow-and-white checkered tea towel.

"Auntie Marge, where is everyone?"

"Well at Grandma's, of course."

"But why did they leave us behind?"

"For goodness sake, Roberta, why would you want to go with them? They're all working on the bomb shelter and Aaron would be underfoot. You were still in the tub when they were ready to go." She turned to face me. "I thought you'd be happier here."

I liked Auntie Marge. I didn't mean for her to think I didn't want to be here. "You're right. Thank you for letting us stay."

I wished Mom and Dad included me in their plans, but they never did. I hadn't known Oma was in the hospital until later, or that Dad was looking for a new job until he got one. They included Tami, but treated me as if I were a baby. I wasn't. They should have asked me if I wanted to stay here or go with them. *I bet they asked Tami.*

Auntie Marge's home was comfy and bright, especially her kitchen. There was a breakfast nook in a circular alcove surrounded by windows with sheer, ruffled curtains. Brightly colored pots of leafy plants squatted on the deep windowsills. I sat on the wooden bench at the yellow chrome table and watched Auntie Marge cover the biscuits in the basket with another tea towel.

Muffy pranced into the room and growled at me. I scooted back on the bench.

"Oh hush, Muff," Auntie Marge scolded. "She won't bother you, Roberta. You leave her alone, she'll leave you alone."

She put on her coat. "I'm going next door for a few minutes. Keep an eye on Aaron."

I nodded, smiling inside. Everyone thought Aaron needed keeping an eye on. It tickled me that my aunt didn't want to leave her house for a few minutes without knowing Aaron was being watched. But if Aaron was going to get into something, I couldn't stop him. All I could do was "keep an eye on him" while he did it.

Muffy barked at the closed door.

"Okay Muffy, you leave me alone, I'll leave you alone." The little dog pattered in my direction, growling and looking at me with her ugly bug-eyes.

I tucked my legs under me. I wasn't afraid of all dogs, but Muffy had nipped at me before, and my aunt wasn't here to order her to "hush."

The small dog's long, silky hair brushed against the floor when she moved—like a fancy dust mop. She had an ugly face with big eyes that protruded too far and bottom teeth that stuck out farther than her top teeth.

She trotted right up to me, yapping and growling. I stood on the bench to get farther away. Muffy's bark-growl grew fiercer and she tried to jump up on the bench, right at my feet. I jerked back hitting against a flower pot. It tumbled off the windowsill onto the bench. Before I could grab it, it crashed to the floor. The pot shattered; shards and dirt spread everywhere. Muffy yelped and raced through the swinging kitchen door.

I froze, too terrified to climb down from my perch in case Muffy returned. But what would Auntie Marge say when she saw the mess I'd made? "Aaron!" *Can he hear me through the kitchen door over the noise of the television?*

He came and grinned at me standing on the bench. "Bertie, what did you do?"

His eyes widened when he saw the broken pottery and dirt strewn across the kitchen floor. Muffy scampered up beside him; he reached down absently and petted her head. I gasped and jumped down from the bench, ready to shoo away the dog if she bit my little brother, but Muffy didn't nip or even growl. Aaron laughed. His blue eyes brightened as he pulled a piece of candy from his pocket and gave it to the little dog. Muffy danced at his feet, eager for another treat as he went to the mudroom for the broom. "Good grief, Bertie, she's harmless."

I took the broom from him, and swept the broken pottery and dirt into a pile.

Aaron jumped up on the bench and quaked from head to toe. "Oh, Bertie, save me." He squealed in a high falsetto. "Oh, I'm sooooo scared!" Muffy barked again, but I was not afraid—not with a broom in my hand.

"Come on, Muffy, come on!" Aaron urged her to jump up on the bench. She couldn't reach him; her barking grew louder and more staccato. The kitchen filled with the sounds of Aaron's urging and Muffy's excited yapping.

"What in the world!" Auntie Marge entered the kitchen. She stood with her hands on her hips, slowly surveying the scene: Aaron standing on the bench, the broken pot and dirt on the floor, and me with the broom in my hand. Muffy quieted immediately. She pranced over to Auntie Marge, then sat accusingly, as if to say, "I had nothing to do with any of this."

Words banged around in my head, begging to be freed, but when I opened my mouth, nothing came out. Aaron jumped down from the bench and stood beside me. I wanted to explain that none of this was my brother's fault, that I'd find a way to pay for the broken pot, but the words would not drop from my head to my mouth.

Auntie Marge took the broom from me and swished the mess into the dustpan. "Aaron, I swear, if you weren't my own sister's son, I'd tan your hide. Now get out of the kitchen and behave yourself."

"But, Auntie Marge—" Aaron began.

"Not another word. Out with you. Go on." She swished at Aaron with the broom and we hustled into the living room.

"I'm sorry. I'll explain it to her."

"She won't believe you. She'll think I had something to do with it."

I knew my brother was set to get into real mischief. We needed to go outside. "Get your coat."

At home we went outdoors whenever we wanted to without asking. I didn't know what my aunt's rules were, so it was safer to ask.

Auntie Marge was peeling apples at the sink when we reentered the kitchen.

"May we go outside?"

"That's a good idea, Roberta. Take him to the park. He can't get into mischief there."

Auntie Marge was wrong. We should have stayed inside.

Chapter 26

The Dog

My aunt and uncle lived one block over and two blocks down from Pioneer Park. When we neared the merry-go-round, I recognized Belinda, a girl from Tami's grade at school. She was there with her twin brothers. The boys were gathering small branches from the storm, piling them around a huge rock, trying to make a fort. Aaron ran to join them. I sat on a swing where I could watch them play.

I didn't know Belinda well, but Tami did. I waited for her to speak to me, but she turned toward four teenage boys playing basketball. Their game was fast-paced and rough; their language rougher. Every time one of them missed a basket, he cursed; every time one cursed he looked over at Belinda and she giggled. *Since when is cursing funny? What show-offs.* Disgusted, I turned away.

Aaron and the twins laughed loudly, completely involved in their game. At least they were having a good time. I listened to their happy play and relaxed as I swung gently back and forth.

A dog rounded the corner of the restrooms. He wandered this way and that, his nose to the ground and tail wagging. He looked harmless, but one could never tell about dogs. A basketball player with wild, curly hair called to him. "Here, Duke! Come here, Duke."

As the dog trotted in the teen's direction, Curly-hair hurled the basketball at him, hitting him squarely on the hind-quarters. The dog yelped and changed directions.

Belinda laughed. "Oh, Bruce, don't hit your dog."

"Come here, Duke. Duke, come!" Bruce called him again.

Duke trotted in his owner's direction. This time the teen picked up a stick and threw it hard. The stick sailed over the head of the dog and hit against a small rectangular shack opposite the basketball court. Duke chased after the stick, found it, raced back to Bruce, and dropped it at his feet. The dog barked and wagged his tail, begging his owner to throw the stick again. Soon all the basketball players took turns seeing how far they could throw it, and each time, no matter where it landed, Duke brought the stick back.

"Hey, Aaron," I called. "Come watch this dog!"

Aaron and the twins ran up and stood beside me. They watched only a few minutes, and then Aaron joined the basketball players as Duke returned with the stick. "Hey, guys, let me throw it."

Bruce grinned and gave the stick to Aaron. He threw it hard, but much too high. It sailed out of his hand and dropped on the roof of the shack. Duke raced to the shed and went crazy trying to get the stick. He jumped up all around the little rectangular hut, and then dug at the soft dirt in front of it.

"Hey, what is this shed for, anyway?" asked one of the basketball players.

Belinda knew. "The Lions Club keeps its prizes and stuff in there. You know, from the carnival on the Fourth of July. My dad's the chairman of the parade and the fireworks."

We watched Duke frantically trying to get to the stick. He couldn't see it, but somehow he knew it was in, or on, the shack. He barked and ran around it in circles. Then he pawed the dirt again.

"Hey, Joe," Bruce asked, "you got anything left over from your lunch?" Joe, the shortest of the group, went to get his lunch sack.

The little shed was not built on a regular foundation; its four corners rested on concrete blocks. The bottom of the padlocked door was slightly off the ground. Duke's owner dropped to his knees and dug under the door with his hands. The dog stopped running around the building and licked his face. Duke obviously adored Bruce, even though his owner mistreated him.

Joe returned with half a sandwich. Bruce had made a narrow gap between the bottom of the door and the loose dirt in front of it. He took the sandwich from Joe, showed it to Duke, and then shoved the sandwich under the door, out of reach of the dog.

"Get it, Duke, get it!"

"Look at the stupid dog dig at the door!" Joe laughed. The other two basketball players exchanged a look and left. I should have taken a cue from them.

Belinda giggled.

Aaron got down on his hands and knees and dug with the dog. When Duke barked, Aaron barked. The dirt flew. The twins got in on the fun and soon the three boys and Duke were jostling and barking and digging in the dirt in front of the door. Duke poked his nose under the door, but he couldn't reach the sandwich. He kept pawing the dirt. Aaron and the brothers mimicked him. In no time they were covered with black dust. It was in their hair and coated their arms, clothes, and faces. They barked and dug and elbowed one another, then barked more.

The hole near the door deepened and Duke stuck his head through it. Whining, he pawed forward, stretching to reach the sandwich. Bruce grabbed Duke's hind legs and pulled him back, but Duke had his prize, and in a gulp the sandwich was gone. Aaron and the twins jumped up, laughing and cheering. "Good ole, Duke!" they cried.

But Bruce wasn't done. "Dig, Duke, dig!"

Duke sat.

The mean teen dropped to his knees in front of the shack. "Duke! Dig!"

Duke waggled over to his master and licked his face. The bully grabbed hold of the dog's ears with both hands and forced his head down until Duke whimpered.

"I said 'dig,' you stupid mutt! Now, dig!"

Duke put a paw on Bruce's arm. He pushed it off, red-faced and breathing hard. He gritted his teeth and turned to the boys watching him and the dog. "Okay, you guys wanna be dogs? Then dig like a dog!" The boys did not move. They stood watching, their faces wary, sober.

Bruce squinted and spoke through clenched teeth. "You'll do what I say or . . ." Belinda stepped forward.

He changed tactics. "Look," he said, smiling. "Inside this shack is a bunch of great loot. You want some? Course you do. So, keep digging until the hole is bigger. Then all we gotta do is slip under the door and take what we want. It'll be easy and we'll all get stuff."

I looked from Aaron to Bruce to Belinda. Someone needed to stop this. It was fun watching the dog dig, but this was going too far. We could push the dirt back now, no harm done. Here was my chance to conquer fear. I remembered my decision not to let fear rule me, and how I had so far failed. Here was another chance. A big chance.

I breathed in sharply, poised to say, "No! We are not going to steal for you!" The words were in my head, I just had to get them out of my mouth. I stared at Bruce. He glared at me through pernicious, squinty eyes, his lips pulled back in a sneer. I closed my mouth and looked quickly away. I could not meet his stare.

Aaron took off his coat and dropped to his knees with the other boys who were digging away. I wanted to call him aside, to reason with him that what he was doing was wrong. I didn't even know I was crying until Joe pointed at me and laughed.

"What a baby!" He shook his head.

Aaron stopped digging and looked at me. He rolled his eyes and went back to work, but Joe didn't leave it alone.

"Is that your *baby* sister?" he taunted.

Aaron sat back on his heels, started to say something, but then redoubled his efforts at digging under the door. Still sniffing, I shuffled over to Aaron and put my hand on his back. Maybe I couldn't talk right now, but I had to do something.

He shrugged my hand off. "Go away, Baby-Bertie."

"You little brat!" The tears dissolved as anger took control. I wanted to kick him, to lash out like I had at the swing after the storm.

Duke sat beside Aaron and whined. I remembered Bruce drilling Duke with the basketball and how mean I thought he was. I wouldn't kick my brother. If it was wrong to hit a dog, it was wrong to kick my brother.

I clenched and unclenched my fists and stepped back from Aaron.

Chapter 27

The Crime

As the hole deepened under the door, Bruce and Belinda held hands watching the diggers. "Oh, Brucie," she pouted, "let's just go."

"No chance!"

Brucie? I had better names for him. *Mean ole Bruce. Bruce the Brute. Bruce the Bully. Bad-boy Bruce.*

"Good work, guys. Now, one of you punks crawl under the door." The twins rose quickly and moved toward Belinda. She shook her head at Bruce. He pointed at Aaron. "Okay, kid, get under the door."

I started to protest, but Belinda interceded. "Hey, look. It's not that big a deal. Think of all the money the Lions Club makes on its silly games. And the stuff in there is just junk anyway."

She leaned toward me and lowered her voice as if sharing a secret with a friend. "If their games were fair, we'd win more of the stuff and it wouldn't all be in there anyway. We're evening up the score. It isn't as if the Lions Club cares about this junk. Look, my dad is the president. Don't you think I'd know if any of this really mattered?"

I sensed a false note in all she said, but I didn't challenge her. Aaron began inching under the door. He wriggled and squirmed and huffed. First his head and shoulders disappeared. Dismayed, I watched as the gap swallowed him whole.

"Hey, get me one of those stuffed dogs so I can give it to my girl." Bruce put his arm around Belinda. She smiled up at him.

Muffled bangs came from inside the shack.

Joe got down on his knees and shouted through the gap. "Hey, kid, are there any firecrackers? Get me some firecrackers!"

Small packages appeared under the door. Joe and Bruce snatched them. "Keep 'em coming," Bruce commanded.

Toys in plastic wrappers materialized. There were water pistols, plastic leis, cap guns with caps, pens with flowers on the top, beaded necklaces, marbles.

"Enough of this junk," complained Joe. "Get some of the good stuff."

"I can't see!" Aaron shouted. "It's dark in here!" His voice sounded far away and hollow, but he shoved more packages under the door.

A car horn startled us. Belinda ran around the corner of the shack where she could see the street; she returned in a hurry. "Come on, you guys. Mom's waiting." The twins stuffed trinkets in their pockets while their sister brushed dirt from their jeans and hair.

"I'll see you tomorrow." Belinda smiled coyly at Bruce, then raced around the shed, twins in tow.

Joe and Bruce filled their coats with loot and took off in different directions. Aaron and I were left alone. If someone came by now, we'd be caught red-handed. Bruce and friends would get off, scot-free.

"Aaron, we have to go. You gotta get out of there." The top of his head appeared in the crevice under the door. "Hurry!" I urged him.

"Help me, Bertie. I'm stuck."

"Can you get an arm out?"

Aaron groaned and writhed. His entire head was out, but just to his neck. He groaned and got one arm and shoulder out. I grabbed it and pulled.

"Ouch! Stop!" He was wedged under the door, his face in the dirt.

"Roberta! Aaron!"

Was that Auntie Marge calling? "Stay here, Aaron, I'll be right back."

"Like I'm going anywhere!"

I ran past the swings and piled-up branches to the corner of the park. Auntie Marge was across the street. "Lunch time, Roberta."

"Okay." I tried to sound cheerful. "We'll be right there." She headed back down the sidewalk, and I dashed to Aaron.

He definitely hadn't gone anywhere.

I dropped to my knees and frantically scraped away more dirt, trying to enlarge the hole for him to squeeze through. Dust coated his eyelashes and he sniveled. "Bertie, don't. You're getting junk in my eyes."

I pulled on his arm again, as hard as I could, while he wriggled and struggled and finally his shoulder and other arm emerged. I pulled on both arms. His shirt tore and his snivel turned into a moan. "Keep pulling," he gasped. When I got his bottom through the gap, he crawled onto his knees, panting. He stood shakily. I brushed away the dust covering his face.

"Stand still and close your eyes."

"They are closed."

I brushed off his shoulders, then his back. A hideous scrape showed through his torn shirt.

What a mess we were in. There was no way to explain Aaron's condition to Auntie Marge without getting both of us in trouble. I brushed dirt off the back of his jeans with more force than necessary.

He stumbled forward, but I didn't let up. When my brushing grew into slapping, he ran a few paces away. I'd never before hit my brother, but right now, I didn't want to just slap him; I wanted to hit him hard, to make him cry.

Aaron sniffed. "I shouldn't have crawled in there, huh."

"No, you shouldn't have!" I screamed at him.

He took a step back. "I'm sorry." Then he turned and shuffled toward the sidewalk.

Droplets of blood showed through his tattered shirt. He was hurt and I had slapped him. "Wait. Don't go to Auntie Marge's yet. Let's think of something." The anger drained away as quickly as it surfaced, but the fear remained.

I looked at the mess outside the shed. "Help me." I shoved packages back under the door. I knew Auntie Marge was expecting us any minute, but we needed to hide the evidence.

Aaron picked up a bright green water pistol and looked at it closely through the packaging. "Wouldn't this be fun in the summer?"

"Aaron!" I pretended to be shocked at him, but I knew how he felt. Mom and Dad never bought this kind of stuff for us. They said it was junk. I picked up a plastic package with a fake ruby ring. Would it be so wrong to keep this one little piece of "junk"? I opened the package and tried on the ring. When Aaron wasn't looking, I slipped it in my pocket. It wouldn't hurt just to put it in my pocket for a while. *I'll put it back later.*

"How about if I ask Auntie Marge if we can eat lunch in the park? You stay outside while I ask." I helped Aaron with his coat. He winced.

"It rubs on my back. It hurts."

"You have to wear it, Aaron. We have to keep your shirt covered."

Auntie Marge agreed to lunch in the park. She put peanut butter and jelly sandwiches in a paper sack along with two apples and four chocolate chip cookies. She didn't seem to think it odd that Aaron didn't come in the house with me.

"You stay out of trouble, now." She smiled and waved at us from the porch as we headed back to the park.

Too late for that.

We ate our lunch at the picnic table farthest from the shed. I didn't feel like talking, but Aaron didn't say anything anyway. When he finished his sandwich, he didn't play on the swings or slide or merry-go-round; he began gathering debris left from the storm. There wasn't much big stuff, just lots of twigs and small limbs. We piled the rubble near the boulder where he'd played with the twins. It felt good to work rather than play, as if we were making up for our misdeeds.

I don't know how long we worked, but the sun was low in the sky when I heard Dad calling us.

"Well, look at the two of you." He pointed to the piles of twigs and rubble as he nodded. "Good job, Roberta. Good job, Aaron."

I'd gotten a nod from my father. A nod and a "good job." How many times had I ached to hear those words, to see pride in his eyes? *Take back the nod! Don't say "good job"!* I couldn't even look at him.

"Hey Dad, this park sure was a mess." Aaron spoke cheerfully, as if nothing in the world was wrong.

"Auntie Marge has dinner ready, let's go." We followed Dad back to the house. I didn't know what would happen when we got inside and Aaron removed his coat. I couldn't think of a plan, didn't know what we should say. It was bad enough that we'd be in trouble, but getting in trouble in front of my aunt and uncle made it doubly bad. Would Dad take us to Uncle Dan's woodshed or wait until we got home?

As we neared my aunt's house, I whispered to Aaron, "Don't take off your coat."

It wasn't much of a plan, but it's all I could come up with. Unfortunately, Aaron either didn't hear me or didn't understand the importance of hiding his torn shirt. He hung his coat in the mudroom along with everyone else's.

The bright kitchen light exposed every bit of grit and grime on both of us. "Aaron, have you been rolling in dirt?" Mom didn't sound happy at the sight of my brother.

"Not rolling in it, Mom. Just playing."

"And working." Dad patted Aaron's shoulder.

No, Dad, don't brag on us. Not about this. I never thought I'd dread hearing praise from my father.

"Roberta, get your hair out of your mouth."

Thanks, Mom. That's more like it.

Chapter 28

Out of Kilter

I KNEW IT WOULD HAPPEN; I JUST WASN'T SURE WHEN. BUT AS Aaron left the kitchen to wash up for dinner, his back to us all, Auntie Marge gasped.

Mom called to him. "Aaron, get back in here."

I glanced at Dad. He watched Aaron, then turned to me. I looked quickly away.

"Aaron, Roberta, in the living room, please." He said "please" but it wasn't a request.

Aaron stood boldly before Dad. I cowered.

"So, explain." Was he talking to me or to Aaron? I couldn't tell without looking at him, but I couldn't meet his eyes.

"What happened at the park?"

I swallowed, took a breath, and waited for the words in my head to settle in some sort of order. Where should I begin? I put my hand in my pocket and felt the ring I had taken. Shame and guilt washed over me. I tried to speak, but choked on my tears.

I knew my constant crying annoyed Dad, and if ever I didn't want to upset him, it was now. *Go back tears! Don't cry, Roberta.*

"Dad," Aaron said, "my favorite blue shirt got torn. Do you

think Mom can fix it? I sure had fun playing in the park." He spoke brightly. "I didn't mean to get so dirty. I think my back got scraped. It kinda stings."

"How did this happen?" Dad turned Aaron's back to him and examined his wound through the jagged tear.

"Digging. Me and those twins. Do you know which ones I mean? We dug good!"

"The twins and *I*. You dug *well*." Dad paused. "How did digging do this?" He looked closer at the scrape.

Aaron's eyes sparkled and enthusiasm gushed from him. "There was this dog named Duke and he was peachy. He could fetch and stuff, and we pretended we were dogs too. When he dug, so did we. We got kinda rough. Did you know dogs have sharp nails? I'm all itchy. Do you think Auntie Marge will let me take another bath before we go home?"

I was flabbergasted. Aaron hadn't lied, but he hadn't told the truth. I'd never have gotten words out like that.

Auntie Marge called from the kitchen, "Dinner's ready."

We joined the others at the table. My opportunity to confess vanished. How easy it had been to let Aaron do the talking. At dinner the adults discussed the lingering effects of the storm, and, as always, what Cuba and the Soviets were up to; no one asked any more about our day in the park.

I hoped we'd go home right after dinner, but Uncle Dan turned on the television. There was nowhere for me to escape, no storeroom in which to hide. I sat on the floor and watched the news. In color.

More missiles had been discovered in Cuba. *Cuba's flag is red, white, and blue? Copy cats!* Military options were being discussed by President Kennedy and his cabinet. *But the minister said the missiles were defensive, surely we can let them defend themselves!* More missile tests were conducted over Johnston Island.

I tried to remember the names of the islands in Puget Sound. Vashon, Bainbridge, Camano, Harstine, Whidbey. That wasn't all of them. Was one of them Johnston Island?

The next day Aaron and I went to Grandma Benson's with the rest of the family. I peeked at her hydrangea bush before we went inside. Someone had pruned it all the same height and taken away the crushed branches. Auntie Marge and Uncle Dan were drinking coffee in the living room with Grandpa Benson, but I didn't see Grandma. I escaped to the familiar kitchen. Aaron was already there, peeking into the cookie jar. I could tell by his face that it was empty. We never knew what kind of cookies might be in it—chocolate chip or peanut butter or oatmeal or snickerdoodle—but it had never before been empty.

"Where's Grandma?" I whispered to Aaron. I don't know why I whispered or why I thought he'd know where she was. He shrugged and put the lid back on the cookie jar.

Mom found us in the kitchen. "You may go outside, or in the basement with the rest of us, but you can't go through Grandma's kitchen without her here. You still have to ask if you want something."

"Where is Grandma?" I hoped Mom knew.

She didn't have a chance to answer because Grandpa Benson grumbled into the kitchen. "The old woman went to church. Said this isn't the time to be skipping services. I say this isn't the time for her to quit doing her job. Gotta get my own coffee, and lunch isn't even started."

I shouldn't have been surprised about the gruffness in Grandpa's voice. The only time I hadn't seen him in a bad mood was the other night with the hydrangea bush. How was it that he could *not* yell at me then, but be upset because Grandma went to church now? I didn't understand. Being in the same room with him made me nervous. I didn't want a slipper thrown at me or curse words hurled my direction.

"Roberta, take your hair out of your mouth." Mom tapped my shoulder, then headed for the basement. Aaron and I followed.

Kerosene lanterns attached to the walls lit the way. The cellar was completely transformed. Tall boards, almost as thick as my thighs, stood on end, encircling the room, and another row divided the basement in half. Plywood lay on top of the boards, creating a new ceiling. On top of the plywood were rows of bricks stacked three and four high. I didn't understand the bricks on the ceiling or the boards down the middle of the room, but I liked the fresh smell of cut wood.

"Dad, why'd you do this?" Aaron pointed up to the ceiling.

"Because it isn't enough to have concrete walls, Aaron. The radiation comes down from above."

I chewed on my hair. *Radiation comes from above. Of course. How am I going to make a safe ceiling in the storeroom?*

Uncle Dan looked critically around the room. "We still need to put in a propane heater and a way of disposing of wastes. Have you any new ideas about a water source?"

Aaron bent down to look into a tube sticking out of the original concrete wall. "What's this for, Dad?"

"Ventilation. Can't live in a closed up room for two weeks without some sort of ventilation."

Two weeks? I needed two weeks of supplies for five of us? I had thought it might be two days, maybe three, but two weeks?

Time was running out; even Dad thought so or he wouldn't skip church to finish this bomb shelter for Grandma. The dirty Commies weren't going to wait until we were ready. I couldn't say, "Hey

Cuba, hey Soviets, could you hold off bombing us until I get this shelter ready?"

Cement ceilings, water, ventilation, heat source, waste disposal. I couldn't do it. I couldn't make the storeroom into a bomb shelter. Nobody could. It didn't even have concrete walls, just thick wooden ones. The Commies would bomb us and we'd suffer beta burns. We'd vomit and die. And there was nothing I could do about it. Grandma Benson and mean old Grandpa Benson would be safe, but Aaron and Tami and I would die.

My eyes smarted with the familiar rush of forming tears, and then, suddenly, I was angry—too angry even to cry. The swelling tears shrank back, and I found my voice. I stomped my foot, glared at my father, and shouted, "What about us? Why don't you care about a safe place for us? I want to live, too. And so does Aaron and Tami and Mom. How can you not care about us?" I finished in a high-pitched scream. It was sassy, sassier than Tami had ever been, but I didn't care. Anger demanded an answer.

The instant I stomped my foot, eight adult eyes stared at me. Dad took slow, deliberate steps toward me. My eyes were riveted on his face, looking for a sign, some signal of his intentions. I did not shrink back when his cool, gray eyes met mine. The anger within me raged. No words rampaged within my head; my mind was clear and focused. I wanted to know why Dad wasn't preparing a bomb shelter for us; why he didn't care if we lived or not. He grasped my arm, walked me up the stairs, and roughly escorted me into the kitchen.

My initial fury softened as Dad pulled out a chair and motioned for me to sit. He rubbed his forehead with both hands as if trying to wipe away unpleasant thoughts. I remained rigid, perched on the edge of the wooden seat.

He dropped his hands onto the table. "Are you calm enough to listen?"

I nodded and breathed deeply, trying to stretch out the small, quick breaths that left me dizzy.

"Look at me."

I stared at the table and began to tremble. The anger and determination dissolved. My chin quivered and the trembles grew until I was a mass of silent, quaking nerves. I didn't hear Aaron come into the room, but I felt him brush against me.

"Dad, will there be room in the shelter for Lincoln Logs?"

"Yes." Dad reached over and lifted my chin, forcing me to look at him. "There will be room for Lincoln Logs, and puzzles, and books. And nine cots."

Lincoln Logs? Puzzles? Books? Nine cots?

"The shelter is for all of us?" The question squeaked out of my tight throat.

I'd never felt so foolish, not even when I ran out of the classroom on the first day of school. "The shelter is for all of us." I repeated the words as I looked in Dad's eyes.

He nodded. Aaron went back downstairs. Neither of us spoke. I removed my hair from my mouth and took a deep breath. "I'm sorry I sassed."

I knew I had to apologize. Not because I'd be in trouble if I didn't, but because I hated the way I felt.

"We'll talk about it later." He paused before going back to the basement as if he wanted to say something else. His piercing eyes locked on mine, but I didn't look away.

"I really am sorry." My chin quivered.

"I know."

I went outside and sat beside the pruned hydrangea bush. The bomb shelter was for me, too. All the special care Dad put into making it safe was for all of us. Why didn't I know that before? It seemed so obvious now. How had I missed it?

What was going on with me? I had sassed Dad, but backed down from Bruce at the park. Why? With a small stick I stabbed the wet dirt, making little round holes in the shape of a square.

I sassed Dad out of anger, but when the anger left, fear reared back up as if it had been there all along just waiting to take over. Were fear and anger related? When one was present, was the other far behind? Could I be afraid of *some* things, but not be ruled by fear? I didn't know. The ideas were too new for me. I jabbed the dirt inside the square with the stick.

The world was out of kilter. It wasn't just that I had yelled at Dad—or that Grandpa Benson hadn't yelled at me. It wasn't just the strangeness at church when people talked aloud in the sanctuary. Those things were big: too big. Big things came and went; they didn't stay. A storm came and left. You cleaned up the damage, but then went on as before. Big things happened, like Christmas when you tumbled out of bed and unwrapped presents before getting dressed, but that didn't *change* anything. It didn't mean that you could get away with not getting dressed before breakfast the next day.

Dampness from the ground soaked through my jeans, but I stayed put by the brown and broken hydrangea bush. My head reeled with the little things that had happened lately, the rules that had been broken. I had left home with my bed unmade. We had left the dishes half done after dinner.

If you could break a rule, and nothing bad happened, then why have the rule?

Maybe it was okay to do something differently from how we

usually did it. An unmade bed did not mean the world was coming to an end. Maybe I didn't have to worry about rules.

Yes, I do! Without rules how could I be sure I was doing the right thing? How could I avoid the woodshed or please my dad if I didn't follow rules? I chewed on a strand of hair. I remembered the stolen ring. Guilt attacked again. I tried to shake it off, but it merged with my fear and confusion until I didn't know how I felt.

Did everyone sometimes break rules? Was everyone afraid sometimes? Maybe it was more a matter of how to deal with fear than not having fear. Rules helped me control my fear; they forced order.

But fear ruled me, regardless of the rules I followed.

Chapter 29

Bull's-eye

MONDAY AFTER DINNER WE TOOK A LOAD OF BOMB SHELTER SUP-
plies to Grandma's. As we pulled up, Grandpa shouted from the
doorway, "Get in here! The president's on TV." The darkened living
room smelled of pipe smoke and lemon oil furniture polish. Their
electricity had come on just before dinner.

I passed behind Grandpa's chair and squeezed between the end
table and arm of the couch. I knew the rules: No Talking Except
During Commercials, and Don't Cross Between Grandpa and the
TV, but what if there were rules I didn't know? I'd never watched
TV with Grandpa in the living room. I perched tensely on the arm
of the couch next to Mom and chewed on my hair. She patted the
cushion next to her and Dad sat, leaning forward, elbows on his
knees. Aaron lay on the floor; Tami sat on a hassock. No one spoke.
They sat and waited and listened. Grandma's rocking chair creaked
softly in rhythm to her gentle movement.

President Kennedy looked solemn. "Good evening, my fellow
citizens."

I covered my heart with my right hand and stood, then realized what I'd done and quickly sat down on the arm of the couch.

Grandma noticed, but didn't say anything. She rocked slowly, calmly. Creak . . . creak . . . creak.

Parts of the speech passed over my head, but some phrases jabbed.

". . . unmistakable evidence has established the fact that a series of offensive missile sites . . ." *No! They are defensive, the minister said so!*

"The purpose of these bases can be none other than to provide a nuclear strike capability . . ."

He didn't stop there, but my heart almost did. Those words, "nuclear strike capability," stabbed my core with panic. Nuclear strike capability in Cuba. It was happening. Nuclear war was closer than ever. Our president was addressing the nation, today, Monday, October 22, 1962, because our world was on the brink of disaster.

More phrases jolted me, like "weapons of sudden mass destruction." *Sudden mass destruction?* Those three words should never go together. I sucked on my braid tip and fought to hold back tears of panic.

I wanted to leave the room, but couldn't move. I wanted Dad to say, "Well, there must be some mistake." Or even Grandpa Benson to curse, "He blankety-blank doesn't know what he's blankety-blank talking about." But they didn't.

The president continued. "Nevertheless, American citizens have become adjusted to living daily on the bull's-eye of Soviet missiles." *No we haven't! We aren't adjusted to living daily on the bull's-eye of missiles!*

"Noooooooo!" I screamed at the television. I leapt from my seat, ran in front of Grandpa Benson's chair, through the kitchen, and down the stairs into the bomb shelter. I sat on the concrete floor in a corner, my back against the wall, knees drawn up, and my hands over my head like we'd been taught at school. I cried and didn't care if anyone heard me. A few minutes later Aaron and Tami joined me. They didn't say anything, didn't try to stop me from sobbing. Aaron sat beside me; Tami sat beside him. They didn't cry, but they did draw up their knees and rest their heads on them.

I fought for control, and when my blubbering settled into hiccoughs, Tami spoke. "Bertie? It's gonna be okay. Everything's gonna be all right."

My sister appeared blurred through my tears. It wasn't like her to comfort me. She teased or ignored me, but she never tried to soothe me. If everything was going to "be all right," why wasn't she teasing me?

After a while adult conversation filtered into the room. "It must be over." Tami rose from the floor. She hesitated before going back up the stairs, but I didn't ask her to stay. After a few more minutes Aaron got up too. He picked up two flashlights from the shelf. "Want to play Flashlight Face?"

Chapter 30

Distractions

THE FOLLOWING TUESDAY, TEN DAYS AFTER THE STORM, THE POWER was restored to all of Thurston County. The morning of the first day back to school dawned gray and wet. I liked rain, I just didn't like getting drenched on the way to the bus stop with no way to dry off quickly. Aaron and I dawdled and our unspoken conspiracy to miss the bus worked; it honked as it passed our lane. Mom donned her coat over her blue-flowered flannel nightgown and drove all three of us to school. A cloudburst timed its downpour to coincide with Tami's stop in front of the high school building.

"I left my coat at home." The rain tap-danced on the street and sidewalk.

"Here, take this." Mom shrugged out of her coat. Tami draped the coat over her head and dashed through the hammering down-pour as Mom drove to the covered walkway near the lower grades' entrance. "Bundle up, Aaron, or you'll be drenched."

"Okay, Mom."

We sprinted through the rain, but I forgot to close the door. Mom tapped on the horn and I raced back, slammed the door, and tore for the walkway. I heard the horn beep again, but I didn't turn around.

Mrs. Pierce and several classmates were standing at the window as I entered the room. A car horn blared.

"Hey, Roberta," John, the boy who sat in front of me, called from the window. "Does your mom drive a red station wagon?"

"Yes." I put a book on my desk.

Another boy snickered. "Does she wear a blue nightgown?"

"What?" I joined the group at the window. There was Mom, standing in the rain in her blue nightgown, the car hood up, and the horn blaring.

"Okay, class, take your seats." Mrs. Pierce turned most of the kids away from the window, but I couldn't stop watching.

Mom pulled the dampened nightgown away from her body and fiddled with something under the hood. A man got out of a pickup, Mom looked at him, nodded, then got back in the car. Seconds later the blaring horn silenced, the man closed the car hood, and Mom drove off.

This was too embarrassing. The entire school probably watched. Maybe the whole town saw her. Why did she get out of the car? Why didn't she just drive away?

The tardy bell rang and class came to order, but bits of laughter interrupted the morning announcements. Finally the noon bell rang and everyone left. I dawdled, pretending to look for something in my desk. I didn't want to face anyone in the cafeteria or at recess in the gym.

Mrs. Pierce stopped beside me. "Roberta."

"Yes, ma'am."

"Tell your mother thanks for what happened today."

"Ma'am?"

"Our country is in the middle of a crisis and I know you are aware of the serious danger we face. I wondered how I would handle class today, our first day back after the storm, only one day after the president's address." She paused and smiled, her eyes mirthful. "The thing with the horn. It took our minds off the crisis. This classroom was free of fear as we began our day and it carried through all morning."

Mrs. Pierce walked away, chuckling.

By the time I entered the cafeteria, the seat next to Carol was taken. I sat at an empty table near the windows. Gray clouds covered the sky, but the rain had stopped. A slight wind jostled tree branches. Someone sat next to me. I turned to see who it was, ready to snap at any comment about my mom.

It was Raul. He unwrapped his sandwich. "Hey."

"Hey." *Why is he sitting here? Was he waiting for me?*

"So, big news this weekend." He took a bite of sandwich.

"Yeah. We watched the president at my Grandma's."

"We watched at home. Kinda scary."

I didn't know what to say next. My palms grew sweaty, my throat dry. I couldn't swallow the bite of food in my mouth. I took a drink to help wash it down. *Why isn't he saying something? Should I say something? Something about Soviet missiles? Or about the storm?*

"Did you have much storm from the damage?" I rushed out the words, then realized I mixed them up.

"I mean did you have . . ."

"Naw, not too much." His smile wasn't *too* big. His eyes didn't laugh *too* much.

Dad had the newspaper ready at dinner that night, but Mom spoke up right after the prayer. "I need you to take a look at the car, Ron."

"Why? What's it doing?" He set down the paper.

"It stalled today when I took the kids to school. It wouldn't start and then the horn got stuck." Mom forked a slice of roast beef onto her plate.

I felt my face burn remembering the kids watching her from the window. Why hadn't she gotten dressed before taking us to school?

"What did you do?"

Maybe she won't tell him the details.

"Harvey Johnson passed by. He got it going again. Pretty quickly, I might add, but I'd still like you to look at it." Mom giggled, then the giggles grew into guffaws. Aaron and Tami laughed.

Dad looked around the table. "What's so funny?'

Aaron spoke up. "It might be that she was standing outside the car in her nightgown in the rain when Mr. Johnson came by."

Mom's laughter increased as Aaron finished the tale, and I smiled at the reminder of how funny she looked.

During dessert, Dad opened the *Dale Valley News* and read the headline, "Vandalism at Pioneer Park."

"Dad," Tami interrupted, "kids at school said the Lions Club storage shed had been broken into, but I thought it was just a rumor."

"Why would someone do that?" Mom shook her head.

It was a good question. Why had I taken the ring? Why hadn't I stopped Aaron? My face burned. I chewed on a strand of hair.

Dad scanned the paper. "It happened Saturday, probably in broad daylight."

It didn't make sense. Why would the paper make a big deal about a few trinkets taken from the Lions Club, when the world was on the brink of war? I answered my own question. It was a distraction, like Mom in her nightgown in front of the school. It gave the community something else to think about. It certainly was giving Dad something else to think about.

Dad looked at Aaron. "They think a dog was involved." He

paused. "Bits of blue fabric were discovered on the bottom of the door."

I spread the mashed potatoes around my plate. When I looked up, his eyes were fixed on me. "So, Roberta, what do you think about this crime at the park?"

I couldn't breathe, but I knew what I had to do.

Chapter 31

In the Woodshed

WITHOUT ASKING TO BE EXCUSED, I LEFT THE TABLE AND WENT TO my room. Aaron followed.

"Bertie, wait."

"Aaron, he knows."

"No he doesn't."

"Even if he doesn't, I have to tell. What we did was wrong. Not telling doesn't make it right."

I retrieved the detestable ring still hidden in my coat pocket. I didn't realize Aaron had stolen anything, but out of his play coat pocket, he pulled the bright green water pistol still in its wrapper.

"Wait, Bertie. You know we're gonna get in a lot of trouble for this."

"You don't have to confess, but I do. I feel so guilty." I put my hand on Aaron's arm. "If we don't tell him, we will have to lie."

Aaron looked in my eyes when I said "lie," and nodded his head. "Yeah, lying is pretty bad." He paused. "Lying is worse."

When we returned to the kitchen, Mom stared at the things in our hands. Tami gawked wide-eyed. Dad stood.

I did what I always did—cried. The tears didn't stream down

silently; I cried aloud. I screwed up my face and bawled. I tried to say I was sorry, but the words gurgled in my throat.

Mom was flabbergasted. "Oh! How could you? I can't believe it! This is just too much." She took a breath and looked from me to Aaron and back again. "How could you?" The anguish in her voice, the disappointment in her eyes, bore into my heart.

When we were at the park, I knew it was wrong to let Aaron enter the shack. But knowing something is wrong is not good enough. *Why hadn't I just walked away? Why hadn't I stood my ground? Why did I listen to Belinda?* I was a dolt, a stupid ignoramus. What good were A's on a report card if I was as brainless as a twit?

Dad signaled for Aaron to wait and for me to follow. I had always been careful not to do any wrong thing because I was terrified of the woodshed. My plan was uncomplicated: if I always did the right thing, if I followed the rules and didn't talk back or misbehave, then I could escape the woodshed. Ohhhhhh! I had tried so hard! Yet I had no one to blame. I had put the ugly, fake ring in my pocket; no one made me. I had stood by while the building was vandalized; I could have told Auntie Marge before the hole was dug.

The bark and wood chips littering the woodshed floor poked my bare feet. Dad pulled the chain attached to a single bulb, but the deep shadows swallowed the feeble light. He stood with his feet spread apart, hands on hips, staring at the rows of chopped wood stacked from one wall to the next. The woodshed smelled of pine, cedar and fir, like Dad's mackinaw and hickory shirt.

He motioned me to sit. I sagged limply on a large, round, wooden block. Tears streamed unchecked, as I waited for what was to come. Tami and Aaron never talked about the punishment in the woodshed, but they didn't have to. Kids at school bragged of whippings they endured in woodsheds, and sometimes showed the welts on their legs left by a thrashing from a willow branch. I knew Dad used his belt because I had seen him unbuckling it as he and Aaron or Tami headed inside.

I sat on the wooden block and made myself look at my father. My eyes grew accustomed to the murky light and I could see his face clearly. There was pain in his eyes, in the way he held his mouth, in his hunched shoulders. This look was worse than his scowl. I wanted to say something, but as usual the words bumped into each other and mixed themselves up. I had hurt my dad. I looked past him at the wall. A wheelbarrow leaned against it; our red racer sled hung above a neatly coiled garden hose.

"Roberta."

I forced myself to look at him, not at his hands, not at his feet, but square in his face. I wanted him to hurt me back. Then we'd be even.

He removed his belt and I stood, ready for my thrashing. "Sit down." I obeyed and waited as the silence shouted my shame.

He finally spoke. "Do you know what you did?"

"Yes, sir."

"I don't think you do. You think you vandalized a building and stole property."

"I did, Dad. That's what I did."

"Yes, that's what you did. But you did more. You did worse."

"I know. I didn't tell you the truth about how we got dirty. I lied. It was the same as lying, wasn't it?"

"Roberta, hush. You need to get this right. Hush, and think. What did you do?"

"I disappointed you and Mom."

"Yes, but what else?"

"I hurt the community by stealing from it?" I didn't think that was the worse thing, but I didn't know what he was after. Maybe hurting the community was worse than hurting your parents.

"You're not thinking, you're grasping for answers. Think. What did you do?"

What did I do? I thought about that afternoon in the park. There was Bruce mistreating Duke, and the boys digging under the door, and the bad language, and stealing trinkets. I had cried, I had been afraid.

Is that what he wants me to confess? That I was afraid? How can he know about my fear? How can I confess it?

"Dad?" My voice wavered. "I think I know, but it's hard to say it."

"Continue."

How can I tell him about my fearfulness? How can I ever please him if he knows what a weak mess I am? We'd never had conversations like this. Yet here I was, on the brink of getting the whipping of my life, and I was going to be frank and honest with my father. This confession would destroy all hope of ever getting a nod, but I had to do it. I had to face the ugly truth.

"Dad." I thought I was ready to begin, but nothing more came. He stood silently waiting.

I tried again. "The thing is . . . the thing is that I'm . . ." I began to blubber. The tears had not stopped streaming since I entered the woodshed, but now hysterical sobbing took control and I couldn't speak. Dad did not put his arms around me and tell me everything would be all right. He remained where he was, quietly waiting for the storm to pass. When the wails diminished to hiccoughs, I tried again.

"I am afraid. I am afraid of everything. I'm afraid of not doing or saying the right thing. I'm afraid of breaking the rules." I choked out the words, my voice heavy with the reality of what I was acknowledging. "I am afraid of Auntie Marge's dog, afraid of nuclear war and how I will get home when the bombs come. I am afraid of being alone and of the wind. I'm afraid of big boys in parks and Grandpa Benson. I'm afraid of Tami's room since Oma died. And I'm afraid of you."

My eyes never left Dad's face. I plead guilty to my crimes and felt the full weight of my shame, but I had to do this right. I couldn't confess to the ground, I had to confess to my father.

"You're getting close," Dad answered. "But you're not there yet. What is behind your fear?"

My mouth dropped in surprise. I don't know what I expected, but his reply was not it. *What does he mean, I am close? Didn't he hear my humiliating list? Doesn't he understand?* Fear of failure, fear of things out of my control, fear of pain, of disappointment, of not measuring up dictated my life! A bit of rebellion sprang up within me. I had just confessed my deepest secret, and he took it, threw it aside, and asked for more. There was no more!

"What is behind your fear?" Dad repeated.

What is behind my fear? He is asking the wrong question. Fear is behind everything. There is nothing behind the fear!

"You've got to do this. You've got to figure this out. I take some responsibility because I've allowed you to grow up without a trip to the woodshed. Now you are here; we have to do this right. This thing behind your fear, you've got to name it. You've got to name it and confess it, not to me, but to God. You've sinned against God; you must answer to Him."

I looked at Dad's face. I peered into his eyes, seeking the answer I couldn't find. I looked, for the first time, deeply into my father's eyes, his intense, piercing eyes and he gazed back into mine. That's how he knew about the fear! He had seen into my eyes even if I hadn't seen into his.

Now I wanted to know the answer as well. "Dad, I don't know. How do I find it?"

He positioned a three-cornered chunk of wood and sat on it beside me. I could see him better, look into his eyes more clearly. My fear of punishment disappeared. The only reality was my father and I sitting together, thinking together. I kept my eyes on his face. A picture of Tami looking and speaking boldly flitted through my mind.

"Tami isn't afraid." Then I thought about Tami comforting Mom after Oma died and how I had felt in the way. Was that a piece to this puzzle?

I remembered that I wasn't afraid to share my deepest thoughts with Oma, but who could be afraid of her? She was all acceptance and warmth.

I searched my dad's face for more clues, but his eyes were cast down. He sat very still. "When are you most afraid?"

"All the time."

"All the time?" He looked back up at me. "You're afraid all the time?"

When am I not afraid? I am not afraid in my daydreams when I am in control and solving the world's problems. *When am I not afraid?* When I have nothing to prove, when I have nothing to risk. When my imagination controls the outcome. When I can change the rules if I want to. The answer came slowly, but it came.

I am behind the fear.

Tami could comfort Mom, because Tami wasn't thinking about herself, she was thinking about Mom. Her life wasn't all about her. She could bring Grandpa Bensen matches, because he needed matches. If he acted inappropriately, then that was his problem, not hers. She could ask to use the camper because she wasn't afraid of a negative answer. If Dad said no, she'd figure out something else.

I hadn't wanted Dad to cry over his mother because of how it made me feel. My selfishness made me feel embarrassed when Mom got soaking wet in her nightgown. Not for a minute did I consider how she felt, cold and wet and humiliated in front of the school. Focusing on self kept me from playing with my family after the storm. Why hadn't I figured this out before?

"Dad, I got it!" I rose from the block of wood and clapped my hands together. "I'm selfish; that's what. All I think about is how something is going to affect me. I think about what people are thinking about me. I worry about me, me, me! That's what's behind the fear, isn't it, Dad? I'm selfish!" I beamed at the success of my discovery.

Dad did not smile. I looked at his grave expression and sat down. The excitement drained from me like water pouring through a sieve.

I am selfish. That is not better than fearful. Being fearful made me feel like a victim, gave me an excuse for my actions. What did selfishness do? Selfishness was ten times worse. Fear was a weakness; selfishness was wicked! Selfishness was sin in a much uglier way than fearfulness was. I put my hands over my face and cried again.

Dad lifted my chin. I couldn't meet his eyes. I couldn't look at him, I was so ashamed. I'd rather he think I was fearful than selfish. There it was again! I was more concerned with what someone thought about me than what was real.

"I am selfish," I sobbed and dropped my head.

"Tell God."

I bobbed my head up. Do what? I stared openmouthed at Dad, but he was looking down, fiddling with a stick of kindling.

I sat on the chopping block and wondered how I was supposed to tell God. Was it the "Our Father which art in heaven," words? I started to recite them.

"No."

This is too hard! I bowed my head and words crashed around inside. I waited. The words sank from my head down to my heart. My head was silent as my heart beat out the words. "I am selfish, God, and I'm sorry."

I looked in Dad's eyes. He nodded, slowly, deliberately.

"I don't want to be selfish."

"Then don't be." He rose to his feet, the stick of kindling still in his hand.

"Stand up."

Here it comes, I thought. If I deserved a spanking for being fearful, I doubly deserved it for being selfish.

Dad took a lighter from his pocket and caught the tip of the kindling on fire. When its tip had turned to charcoal, he wrote large, black letters on the chopping block: S E L F I S H.

He put down the stick, picked up his belt, doubled it, and handed it to me. "Beat it," he said.

"What?"

"Beat the selfishness. Whip it. Go on." He nodded at the block.

I hit the block halfheartedly with the belt.

"Is that what it deserves?"

I looked into his cool, steel-gray eyes and saw what I'd never noticed before. My father loved me enough to hate my weakness. He wanted my weakness beaten, not me.

I struck the block viciously again and again. I walloped the "selfish" etched on the block, staring at me, accusing me. I saw the bold, black letters and despised them. I whacked the word over and over, every strike a blow against this horrid weakness that was mine. I couldn't speak for weeping, as my heart screamed, *I hate you! I hate you! I hate you!*

When the letters were obliterated and my arms weary, Dad took the belt from me. I thought we were done. I was wrong.

"With what will you replace the selfishness?"

I was worn out; I couldn't think. I couldn't search for any more answers. But this time the answer was obvious because it lived in my father's eyes. The answer was *love*. I would replace selfishness with love.

Chapter 32

Wind and War

DAD DROVE AARON AND ME TO THE EMERGENCY LIONS CLUB MEET-
ing on Sunday afternoon. Aaron clutched his water pistol and I carried my fake ruby ring. We did not hide them in a paper sack, but
held them in plain sight.

Dad opened the massive, mahogany double doors; he walked
behind us as we entered the room. The hardwood floor creaked as
we approached the men wearing suits and sitting at a bulky, dark
table in high-backed chairs. Belinda's father sat at the head of the
table. Did he know her part in the escapade? He lectured us about
the destruction we had caused and sentenced us to working every
Saturday for a month at the park. He did not ask us questions or
allow us to make any statements. I stood with my head bowed as
his stern words washed over me, but I did not cry. When he was
done reprimanding us, we placed the pilfered items on the desk
and exited.

That evening while Dad watched the news, I knocked on Tami's
door.

"Come in."

I turned the doorknob and entered the room in which Oma had

died. A nameless fear had kept me out, but I had defeated fear when I confessed selfishness. The door to love was open.

I sat on the edge of the bed, just like I had done when Oma was there. Tami lay on her stomach looking at hairdos in a fashion magazine. "Oh, I like that one." I pointed to a poufy style that flipped up on the ends. Then I noticed it was exactly how Tami wore her hair. "I'm lucky you're my sister." The words came out unplanned, catching me as unaware as they did Tami, but they were still true. Tami was nothing like Belinda. If Tami had been at the park, she'd have stood up to them all. She'd never think cursing was something to giggle at. She'd not stand by and watch a dog get hit with a ball or a bully force little boys to crawl under doors.

Tami twisted onto her side and faced me. After a second of silence, she sat up and slid to the floor. She ducked under the bed and came up with the box containing her script.

"You read so much, Bertie. You know about books and writing. Could you tell me what you think about this? I know it isn't a book, but it's still writing. Mom's going to want to see it, but if you read it first and tell me what you think . . ."

"I'd love to!" I took the box from her. "Can I start now? What's it about?" I hugged the box to my chest.

Feelings overpowered and silenced me. Joy splashed around in my heart, but wouldn't bubble up to my mouth. It didn't matter. I didn't fight for words. I looked at my sister, then back at the box in my arms, and smiled. She smiled back, and that was words enough.

The next day, I walked home from school so I could think more. A convoy of army jeeps rumbled by on the highway. I wondered how the army men felt. Were they afraid? Things were going from bad to worse. What would it mean to be in the army during times like this? I hurried down the tracks, eager to get home.

I changed into play clothes, slipped into the woodshed, and sat on the chopping block. Mice made small scurrying sounds among the pieces of wood. Poor mice. Afraid to come out in the open, made to hide under wood piles.

Am I a mouse? As fearful as a mouse?

Selfishness triggered most of my fears, but how did selfishness cause fear of wind or war? I wasn't selfish to want to live. Perhaps I was silly for wanting a light-colored coat, but it wasn't selfishness. And how did selfishness relate to the panic I felt when wind rustled through the trees? I lingered in the gathering darkness, no closer to an answer. The clanging triangle called me back into the house.

During dinner Aaron told about the marbles he'd won at school and Mom complained about the cold nights. Dad brought up the Soviets, but he didn't read from the paper. "Heard that Khrushchev authorized dismantling the missiles in Cuba. He announced it yesterday in a speech aired on Radio Moscow."

"Does that mean the crisis is over?" I spoke before thinking, but my words came out clear and not jumbled together.

"Yes, this crisis is over." Mom sighed.

After the dishes were done, I approached Dad in the living room. "Can we go to the woodshed?"

"*May* we go. No. The woodshed is for discipline. The living room is fine for conversation."

"Okay." I sat on the hassock in front of Dad's easy chair. Mom put down her mending, and Tami looked up from her homework. This was new territory. I didn't sit in the living room in the evening with my family or participate in discussions. What were the rules for this?

"Okay," I said again. *Can I get more words out? What if I scoot the hassock closer and speak softly so only Dad can hear?* My eyes watered, and I almost gave up. I sighed and glanced at my father. He watched me with a steady, confident, calm look.

Mom returned to her mending.

I breathed deeply. "Here it is. I'm afraid of nuclear war and hurricanes." I looked at Dad as I spoke. "Love does not stop war; love does not control the wind. I'm afraid, but I don't think this is selfishness. I have the light-colored coat, but it's not always with me and I don't have a radio so how will I know if there is a storm and even if there is one, what do I do?"

Dad remained quiet. Tami mumbled her confusion. "Huh? A light-colored coat?"

"That's not the point," I persisted. "Dad, are you afraid of nuclear war? Are you afraid of hurricanes?"

Would he answer my direct question? In the past I would have backed off for fear of sassing. I knew I was still focusing on myself, but I needed this answer.

After an eternity Dad spoke. "You are wrong, Roberta. Love does control wars. Love does control the wind." He returned to reading the paper and I knew he meant for me to figure it out.

After I went to bed, I lay awake thinking. History showed that warmongers viewed love as weakness. Love did not stop evil men from exploiting the poor. Power hungry, ambitious men did not respect love, nor back down because of it. Who could control such men? Certainly no one I knew. I understood that the men at the café and Dad and Mr. Swansen talked about war and destruction because they knew what could happen. Were they afraid?

What did grown-ups do when they were afraid? When Mom waited for news about the loggers, she prayed. Dad and Mom prayed together before the storm. Did the Swansens pray?

I closed my eyes and prayed. I didn't start with "Our Father which art in heaven." I jumped straight to the question on my heart. "Dear God, what about wars and wind? What do I do about them?" I drifted off to sleep as I waited for the answer. The massive hand from my daydreams reached down and plucked me from my bed. I snuggled in the safety of a wool plaid pocket and journeyed on a path through the stars. It was only a dream, but when I awoke I had my answer.

It was cold when I left for school, so I buttoned my light-colored, calf-length, hooded coat, but I knew I didn't need it to live. Dad was right. Love does control the wind and wars.

I wondered if Dad knew that sometimes Love wears a red-and-black plaid mackinaw.

About the Author

BARBARA TIFFT BLAKEY IS A FREELANCE WRITER AND AUTHOR OF the award-winning literature-based language arts program Total Language Plus. Barbara is also a nationally recognized speaker, conducting workshops and seminars for Christian women's groups and homeschooling conventions for more than fifteen years. She lives in Olympia, Washington, with her husband, Terry.